Justin Verner was born and raised in the countryside of northeast Ohio, where he loved playing golf. Solitary hours on the course provided inspiration. He currently resides in the Sonoran Desert in the state of Arizona.

Justin enjoys writing songs, as well as books. He looks forward to a life with Jesus Christ at the forefront.

Justin Verner

JASON AND CATALINA

AUSTIN MACAULEY PUBLISHERS™

LONDON • CAMBRIDGE • NEW YORK • SHARJAH

Ordering Information
Quantity sales: Special discounts are available on quantity purchases by corporations, associations, and others. For details, contact the publisher at the address below.

Publisher's Cataloging-in-Publication data
Verner, Justin
Jason and Catalina

ISBN 9798891551732 (Paperback)
ISBN 9798891551749 (ePub e-book)

Library of Congress Control Number: 2023923110

www.austinmacauley.com/us

First Published 2024
Austin Macauley Publishers LLC
40 Wall Street, 33rd Floor, Suite 3302
New York, NY 10005
USA

mail-usa@austinmacauley.com
+1 (646) 5125767

Chapter 1

Jason woke before dawn, as was his custom. His eyes blinked out the last bits of sleep as he gazed up at the ceiling fan. A smile crossed his face. This was the first morning in his new home. A beautiful home at the foothills of the mountains. Jason decided to call his new home Morning Glory.

He rolled out of bed, threw on a shirt and shorts, and proceeded to the kitchen for his cup of coffee. The hardwood was cool to the touch beneath his feet. He placed two hearty scoops of grounds in the new coffee maker, flipped the switch, and made his way to the front window while his cup was brewing.

In just about an hour, the sun would bless the landscape with twilight. Until then, Jason was in a world all his own. Darkness, silence, and his thoughts. As a novelist, he loved that inner world. It's where imagination takes hold.

And although he was a writer, it had been nearly six years since his name had graced the bestsellers list. A career that started hot out of the gate had now stalled. Jason refused to accept the fact that he was now a has-been at the tender age of thirty-six! *The mid-thirties are supposed to be the fertile stomping grounds!* Yet here he was, six years removed from his last successful piece of fiction.

But then, a feeling of gratitude washed over him. A feeling of pride. His hard work had afforded him this very scene. Novels about Old West gunslingers, camouflaged snipers in the trees, alien visitors from other dimensions, and lonely writers in the City of Angels.

Unfortunately, life imitated art with the last novel. Jason found himself burned out by the L.A. lifestyle. Fast cars and fast girls inflated his ego, but left him lonelier by the year. He realized he wasn't your typical object of sympathy and he never so much as grumbled. Inside, however, he knew it was time for a change before the City of Night took his very soul.

The coffeemaker let out a loud sputtering noise, signaling the brew was complete. Jason snapped himself out of his trance and made his way to his fresh cup. He added a little cream and a few teaspoons of sugar. Soon, the sun's unmistakable glow would be seen peeking over the horizon. His beautiful new home had a wonderful view in all directions, but especially the east.

Morning Glory, as he called it, was a modern A-frame with glorious front windows and a wooden deck on the second level, which surrounded the house on all sides. On the lower level, there was a main door inside the garage. After ascending a flight of stairs, one would arrive in the main living area.

A two-piece sofa sat in one corner of the room and a counter wrapped around the kitchen.

Majestic wooden planks could be seen on the ceiling above, coming to a point and forming the 'A' shape. The large front windows were also cut to this shape, granting visitors an unobstructed view of the mountain that stood before them to the east. Morning Glory was equipped with a set of stairs on each side of the house, allowing guests to ascend from the ground level to the deck above. A door near the kitchen allowed one to enter Morning Glory from the deck.

Hard work and dedication to his craft had provided Jason this wonderful new view. He consciously stopped for a moment to reflect on his good fortune. He always felt someone or something looking out for his best interests. A guardian angel of sorts that hung with invisibility in the ether.

Jason was raised in the Catholic church, which clearly identified this force and associated feeling as the Holy Spirit. But Jason couldn't be sure of it. Although many blessings had been bestowed upon him, his personal relationship with God was strained. But maybe that would change? Maybe that's what really brought him to Morning Glory?

The eastern horizon began to glow orange and Jason smiled once again. He opened a door leading to the deck and felt a rush of cool morning air. He filled his lungs with the pure air and exhaled deeply. Pulling up a chair and placing his coffee on a nearby table, Jason sat and took in the wondrous view before him.

Geographically speaking, Morning Glory lay at the foothills of Humphreys Peak just north of the city of Flagstaff, Arizona. The Coconino Forest was nearby, with its ponderosa pines and aspen groves. And it was Humphreys Peak that stood before him to the east, the tallest peak in all of Arizona. It was paradise, and Jason was beginning to feel it.

The sun officially rose over the horizon at that moment. The dawning of a new day, to be sure. Jason took a few sips from his cup. The caffeine gave him a kick which all but eliminated any cobwebs that were still hanging from the previous night's sleep.

While looking eastward, he noticed a large hill. He was told by the realtor who secured the property that beyond the hill, on the far side, was a lake. A serene lake which sits at the base of Humphreys Peak.

The sun was now fully on display in the morning sky. Birds began to busy themselves with their avian tasks. Other than their chirping, the sound of silence permeated the mountain air. Jason took another sip of coffee.

Morning Glory was the last house at the end of a cul-de-sac. The last house at the end of a dirt road. A dirt road which branched off from the only highway that ran through this community on the outskirts of Flagstaff.

There were several other houses on each side of the dirt road. Mostly humble little ranch houses that had been there for decades. His A-frame was the latest addition to the community.

He wondered what the locals would think of him. A writer from L.A. on a spiritual retreat.

Would they laugh? Would they even care?

Just then, Jason witnessed a glow around the hill that sat before him to the east. Surely it was just the sun illuminating the outline. Or was it?

He looked to his left in an effort to readjust his vision, but when he returned his gaze to the hill, it was still aglow.

The outline of the hill seemed to pulsate and the glow became more intense. Jason was awestruck and frightened at the same time. Was he really losing his marbles on the very first day at his new home? He looked down into his coffee cup, which was nearly empty, and looked back up again.

This time, the glow was gone. The outline of the hill remained still. Jason looked from side to side and let out a deep sigh. A strange sense of calm then washed over him. His initial fright was quickly replaced by serenity.

At that moment, something called Jason. It came from the direction of the hill. It wasn't a voice, but instead more of an internal feeling. In his mind's eye, he began to move across the landscape. He moved eastward toward the hill in his imagination. He was then elevated to a bird's eye view. Sure enough, beyond the hill was a lake. A serene lake which sat at the base of the tall mountain peak. The peaceful feeling that the lake inspired was almost too much to bear.

At that moment, he snapped out of his daydream.

What was that? He tried to shake the feeling but something wouldn't allow it.

Something told him that he needed to explore the lake. He needed to walk to the water's edge. That was all he knew. He proceeded to finish his cup of coffee and walked back inside the house.

After showering and brushing his teeth, Jason dressed himself in the master bedroom. He put on a clean shirt and shorts and laced up his athletic shoes. He made his way down the steps to the garage. Sunshine and mountain breeze greeted Jason as the garage door slowly opened.

He stopped for a moment and took notice of the hill. Beyond which would be a lake at the base of Humphreys Peak. A serene lake. It was calling him. There was no denying the feeling at this point. He didn't even seem to care that the hill and lake were not on his property.

That was an afterthought.

I could be shot dead for trespassing! He knew there was an inherent risk, but the hill beckoned him. The lake on the other side beckoned him. He had to follow the feeling.

Jason traversed the dirt road on foot and passed the humble ranch houses along the way. The second-to-last house on the right had a yellow Jeep parked in the driveway. He kept walking.

About a mile down the road he came to a barbed wire fence. Beyond the wire fence was the hill. He looked over both shoulders and took a running start. Before he reached the fence, he stopped abruptly. The barbed wire was set just high enough to deter such a bold move.

Just then, the top wire snapped before his very eyes! He looked over both his shoulders again, but he saw no one around. Jason looked back to the fence and sure enough, the top wire, which was once waist-high, was hanging limp in two separate pieces. His strange morning just got stranger. A sign from above?

Jason took a large step over the remaining two barbed wires which were still stretched tight across the wooden posts to his left and right. With not a soul in sight, he continued toward the majestic hill which stood before him.

Although it was no longer glowing, the hill still emanated a tranquility which Jason could fully perceive. He continued up the hill, reaching the top in less than a minute.

The view from atop the hill was breathtaking. Sure enough, as he looked down to the other side, there was a lake seated at the bottom.

He continued down the hill toward the lake. As he reached its banks, he stood in a mixture of mud and stone. The water was still, undisturbed. A few birds sailed over the water.

Jason looked to the other side of the lake, to the opposite bank. He saw nothing. But just then, the strange feeling came over him. Frightening at first, then yielding to peacefulness. An inner tranquility.

With his gaze fixed intently on the opposite side of the lake, he noticed something. It was a cross! A cross made of wood, standing nearly ten feet tall! *A mirage! It has to be a mirage!* But the mirage would not dissipate. It just stood there, with Jason as witness.

The wood which made up the cross was a light color, like pine. It was planted firmly in the banks of the lake, as if it had been there for years. Suddenly, it began to give off a natural radiance, much like the hill. And just like that, it was gone.

"No, no!" Jason shouted out loud. "Where'd it go?"

The opposite side of the lake was now empty. The ground on which the cross had just stood looked untouched.

"I can't believe this," Jason whispered.

After about a minute of standing in bewilderment, Jason turned around and began to head home. Over the hill and back to Morning Glory.

When he returned, he entered through the garage and proceeded up the stairs. As he made his way into the main living area, he noticed a book on one of the end tables near his two-piece sofa. It had not been there earlier. Drawing closer, he could see it was clad in a brown leather cover.

Holy Bible.

That evening, Jason poured himself an ice-cold beer into a pint glass. He grabbed a pair of binoculars in his other hand and headed out onto the deck.

The street was just as quiet as it had been that morning. Not a soul in sight. As he pulled up a chair, he set the binoculars down at his side. He brought the ice-cold beer to his lips and took a healthy swig.

"Ah!" he exclaimed.

At that moment, he spotted a yellow Jeep coming down the dirt road at a decent clip. A cloud of dust was kicked up behind the vehicle. He recalled seeing that very same Jeep earlier in the morning. It was parked in the driveway of the second-to-last house on the right (his house being the last house on the street, at the end of the cul-de-sac).

He set his lager down and proceeded to pick up his binoculars. Raising them to his face, he began to search for the oncoming Jeep with his magnified lenses. He moved the binoculars left to right, then up and down, before finally steadying his hand. *There it is!* He centered his sights on the vehicle.

In the driver's seat sat a most beautiful woman. Adorned with Aviator sunglasses, her gaze was fixed on the road ahead. She bounced up and down with each bump in the dirt road. Her hair was long and black and pulled into a ponytail. Her skin was naturally tan, a golden brown. And her lips were full and plump, with a pout that was ever-so-slight.

The yellow Jeep raced closer and closer to the second-to-last house on the right. Jason kept the binoculars affixed to his face, so as not to miss a single second of the action. The Jeep made a wide turn into the driveway and slowly came to a stop. A euphoric feeling came over Jason.

The driver then opened the door slowly and gently stepped out onto the pavement. She stood tall, with long legs and perfect posture. Her breasts were full and her waist slim. Her bottom was perfectly shaped. It seemed today was a day of visions for Jason!

Just then, through his binoculars, Jason saw the beauty turn her head. She began to look directly at him!

In a quick move, Jason threw the binoculars to the ground. Luckily, they did not go over the railing. A feeling of embarrassment washed over him. His face became flush. He had been spotted! The watcher was being watched!

Jason saw the beauty proceed to her house. Just as she was about to enter, she turned around in place and looked back in his direction. She held her gaze for a moment, chuckled, and then went in through the front door.

Busted!

The first day had come to a comical end.

Chapter 2

The second day at Morning Glory began very much like the first. Jason woke before dawn and shuffled into the kitchen for a cup of jo. As it was brewing, Jason noticed the Bible still sitting on the end table near his two-piece sofa set. A feeling of gratitude filled him from head-to-toe as he looked down at the book.

As he went to pick it up, Jason could feel a soft current of electricity flow through his body. The moment he touched the Bible, the current became more intense. He threw his hands back in shock.

"What the heck?" Jason muttered. He reached out to grab it again, but once again the current of electricity shocked him as he laid his hands upon the Bible.

"Whoa! Okay, fine." Jason stepped back and could hear the coffee maker sputtering.

He turned around, added cream and sugar to his coffee, and headed outside to the deck.

Dawn was breaking and the familiar orange glow could be seen just over the horizon.

The last of the night-time stars began to dissipate in the sky.

As he sipped his coffee, he looked over his shoulder at the Bible sitting on the end table inside his house. Jason never remembered unpacking any books after he arrived. In fact, he was almost certain that all the books he brought with him were still sealed in cardboard boxes inside his garage. Now, the Holy Bible had somehow made its way to an end table in his living room and was charged with some sort of electrical current.

He looked forward again and witnessed the heavenly ball of fire creeping ever-so-slowly above the horizon. He took another sip of coffee and cleared his throat.

In front of him stood the hill, beyond which was the lake, beyond which was the mountain. For a moment, he visualized the events of the prior morning. Ascending the hill, descending the hill, and reaching the water's edge. Then, witnessing the cross just across the water.

He broke from his daydream and looked out toward the hill. It looked normal, slowly being bathed in more and more sunlight. And then, it happened again!

The outline of the hill began to pulsate and glow with increasing intensity. The hill appeared to grow larger, then smaller, larger, and then smaller again. Jason was awestruck, unable to divert his stare. The familiar feeling of fright mixed with tranquility overtook his entire body. For several seconds, he was unable to move.

Then the vision ceased. Normalcy returned to the landscape. Jason looked around to his left and then to his right, but not a soul was in sight. No one to confirm what he had just seen. He looked down the road, to the second-to-last house on the right. The yellow Jeep was parked in the driveway, but the beauty was nowhere to be seen.

Then, another feeling came over him. This feeling was more mental, rather than physical. A small voice inside urged him to return to the lake. This time, making his way around the lake to the other side, where he had witnessed the cross appear just yesterday. The small voice was not audible but communicated the idea perfectly to Jason. It couldn't be reasoned with. He *knew* what he had to do next.

After showering, Jason put on clean clothes, laced his athletic shoes, and headed to the lake. He stepped carefully over the barbed wire fence (with the top wire hanging loose in two separate pieces). He climbed up the hill and walked slowly down the opposite side. He approached the lake and stopped just as he came to the water's edge. Standing there for nearly a minute, he eagerly anticipated a vision. But none came.

He remembered the instructions he was given: go to the other side of the lake. Go to the spot where the cross appeared yesterday morning. And so he did.

Moving to his left, he followed the curvature of the lake to the opposite side, all the while keeping a look out for any vision that might spontaneously appear. When he reached the banks on the other side, he stopped and looked down. The mud and stone mixture was level, untouched. No evidence of a giant cross standing in that very spot could be perceived. And then, it happened.

Out of nowhere, the cross appeared once again! Jason took several steps back in shock. The cross, standing nearly ten feet tall, made of light-colored wood, had manifested itself in an instant. It stood firmly on the banks of the lake. Jason was captivated by the image.

Suddenly, the cross began to radiate a heavenly glow. The glow became more intense and began to pulsate, much like the hill. Jason tried to take a few more steps back, but he quickly realized that he was frozen in place. He couldn't move his legs and he couldn't take his eyes off the glowing cross.

At that moment, a silence fell over the land and Jason witnessed something that left him spellbound: the body of Jesus Christ appeared on the cross! Atop his head rested a crown of thorns. Nails had been driven through his hands and feet. Jason's eyes grew wider than they had ever been before. He stood frozen.

As he looked on mesmerized at the image of Christ Jesus crucified, he began to cry. His heart ached. He batted his eyelids to keep the tears from welling up.

"Thank you," Jason whispered.

The image of Christ Jesus slowly vanished. Jason's tears ceased and he could see clearly.

The ground that had just supported the cross and Christ Jesus appeared undisturbed, untouched. He remained spellbound. He knew he had been changed forever. Jason then made his way back to Morning Glory.

That evening, Jason poured himself an ice-cold beer and headed out to his deck. He was still caught in the afterglow of what he had witnessed that morning. Still in shock. He put the pint glass to his lips and took a healthy swig.

In the distance, he could see a vehicle approaching. From the lone highway that ran through the town, the vehicle turned onto the dirt road. As it raced down the dirt road, a cloud of dust was kicked into the air behind it. The yellow Jeep. The golden beauty.

Jason did not bring his binoculars with him on this particular evening. He had already been caught in the act, so to speak. He took another gulp from his glass and followed the Jeep intently with his eyes.

Much to his surprise, the yellow Jeep passed the second-to-last house on the right and continued toward his house! The beauty in the driver's seat looked in his direction and smiled ever so slightly.

She then pulled into his driveway and came to a stop. Jason couldn't believe what he was witnessing. With so many visions appearing around him recently, he didn't know if this was really happening or the byproduct of an overstimulated imagination. Before he could think about it any further, the beauty stepped out of the Jeep and introduced herself.

"Hi!" she exclaimed.

"Hey there," Jason replied.

"You must be the new guy!"

"I am! My name's Jason. I just moved—"

"I know," she interrupted. "You're Jason Morrison, the famous writer."

Jason smirked. "Well, *formerly* famous writer," he corrected in an attempt at self-deprecation. "It's been a few years since—"

"Right!" she interrupted again. "*Formerly* famous writer."

Jason, caught by surprise, squinted his eyes and pouted his lips. *Is she messing with me? Is she trying to outfox the fox?* He gazed at her with a deadpan gaze. And she, much to his surprise, returned his gaze with a deadpan gaze of her own.

"What's your name?" he asked with confidence.

"Catalina," she replied. "I live in the house just over there." She turned her body and pointed in the direction of the second-to-last house on the right. "But you probably already knew that."

Jason was taken aback at her charm, humor, and, of course, her physical beauty.

Catalina… what a great name.

"Hey," he started, "would you like to grab dinner sometime?"

Something about Catalina attracted him immediately. Something in her way caused him to act boldly, swiftly.

"Sure!" she exclaimed. "How about tomorrow? Do you know where Rocky's Diner is?" Jason nearly melted in place. She liked him!

"Tomorrow's great. But no, I'm not sure where Rocky's Diner is exactly."

"Take the highway south for about twenty miles. Then, turn left on Locust Street. It's about a mile down on the right-hand side. Where's your ride?" she asked inquisitively, staring into an empty garage.

"Funny you should ask," Jason began, "it's being delivered in two days. A new black Challenger." He knew this would impress her.

"Cool," she replied nonchalantly. "Guess I'll have to drive. Be ready at seven." She seemed unphased by the thought of a new muscle car being delivered to his doorstep.

"Seven it is! Bye Catalina!"

"Bye Jason!"

And just like that, she was gone. She climbed into her yellow Jeep, started it up, and went back to her place. Jason watched her walk to her front door. She paused briefly, then turned around and gave him a smile.

Catalina. Oh, senorita!

Chapter 3

Day three at Morning Glory would also begin before dawn. Jason had been sleeping well despite all the heavy events that had been taking place around him. After preparing his cup of jo, he looked over at the Bible on the end table. He walked over slowly and set his mug down.

He was hesitant to touch it; he remembered what had happened yesterday. He feared a similar current of electricity would greet him if he dared to pick it up. However, today Jason felt different. A sense of calm permeated his being as he stood over the Bible.

Without thinking, he reached down and picked it up with both hands. No shock. He let out a sigh of relief. Jason then opened to the Gospel according to John. His eyes were drawn to chapter 1, verse 29, which he read aloud:

The next day he saw Jesus coming toward him, and said, "Behold, the Lamb of God, who takes away the sin of the world!"

Jason was familiar with the story of John the Baptist first laying his eyes on Christ. John knew that Jesus would appear to him one day, and when he did, he was to be exalted. The light of the world!

Jason closed the Bible and placed it back on the end table. He smiled contentedly, feeling as though a weight had been lifted from his shoulders. He picked up his coffee and went out to the deck.

On this morning, the hill to the east did not glow or beckon him. The lake beyond the hill did not call to him either. And even the great mountain peak beyond that hill, beyond that lake, remained silent on this particular morning.

Instead, Jason felt as if he should visit the nearby park. He had not been there since moving in and figured it would be a nice change of pace. He wanted to explore the wilderness that was all around him. The park was just a mile or so down the highway. And so, it was decided.

The park allowed him to retreat into nature. Ponderosa pines reached towering heights, their branches swaying in the breeze. He ran along the path with a smile across his face. He began sweating; his heart began beating faster.

Jason then came upon an aspen grove. The white bark stood out among the surrounding vegetation. He began running through a maze of white tree trunks. *This is just what I needed,* he thought to himself.

Jason came to a stop along the side of the path. He closed his eyes and drew in fresh air through his nose. Holding it for a few seconds, he then exhaled through his mouth. Jason did this several times while keeping his eyes closed. His heart began to beat slower.

Just as he opened his eyes, a bright light flashed before him! He recoiled, holding his hands out in front of his face. As he lowered his hands, an angel appeared!

The angel floated in mid-air about six feet off the ground. It was a female angel, with soft white skin and curly blonde hair. Jason was mesmerized and could do nothing but stare.

"Do not be ashamed!" the angel commanded.

A tear ran down Jason's cheek and he dropped to his knees. The angel was surrounded by a brilliant white aura. He had never seen such a soothing sight in all his life!

"Don't be ashamed of *what*?" he asked.

Just then, the angel began to slowly disappear into the air.

"No, no, please! Don't go!" Jason pleaded.

With each passing second, the beautiful angel slowly faded. Jason, still on his knees, pleaded once more.

"Please! Don't be ashamed of *what*?"

And just like that, the angel was gone. A simple command was all she had to offer. Her utter radiance was something Jason would never be able to forget.

Jason then rose to his feet and wiped the tears from his face. He walked the remainder of the trail, then down the highway, and then along the dirt road which led to Morning Glory.

He walked up the stairs on the side of the house which led to the living area on the second floor. As he opened the door to his new home, he let out a deep sigh. He was exhausted.

Jason headed to the shower.

As he emerged and began drying himself, Jason was still caught in an afterglow. He moved to the master bedroom and collapsed on the bed. A few seconds later, he was in a deep slumber.

❖

Jason woke nearly three hours later and walked into the kitchen well-rested. He glanced down at the Bible on the end table and decided to read a passage. He opened to the Second Letter of Paul to the Corinthians, and read aloud from chapter 10, verses 7 & 8:

Look at what is before your eyes. If anyone is confident that he is Christ's, let him remind himself that just as he is Christ's, so also are we. For even if I boast a little too much of our authority, which the Lord gave for building you up and not for destroying you, I will not be ashamed.

There was that word again: ashamed. The angel told him not to be ashamed. And now he was reading a letter from the Apostle Paul, who was not ashamed to proclaim the glory of Christ.

Jason felt a current of electricity run through his hands as he held the Bible. This time, he did not recoil. He simply let it pass through his body. It was powerful and gripped him completely.

At seven o'clock sharp, Catalina pulled into Jason's driveway and honked her horn. Jason grinned as he descended down the stairs on the side of the house. He opened the passenger door and hopped into the Jeep.

Catalina looked stunning. Her long black hair flowed down her back. She was wearing it in a ponytail again. Her eyes were a deep brown. Her lips were full and red. And her skin was golden, radiant.

"Hey!" Jason said enthusiastically.

"Hi," Catalina replied softly.

Catalina pulled out of the driveway and headed south down the highway to Rocky's Diner. Once they arrived and were seated in their booth, Jason and Catalina began to converse.

"So a Dodge Challenger, huh?" Catalina remarked.

"Yeah. Very American. Classic look. Bad to the bone."

"And you say they're delivering it tomorrow?" she asked.

"Yep. Dealership says they're dropping it off in the morning." Catalina grinned ever so slightly.

Just then, the server came by and took their drink orders. Catalina ordered a Coke. Jason ordered one as well.

"So is that *you*, then? Classic? Bad to the bone?" She kept her gaze fixed on Jason. He returned the favor and looked deeply into her eyes.

"I think so," he replied.

The tension was building. It could be cut with a knife. And just then, the server returned with two Cokes. And took their dinner orders. Catalina chose spaghetti and meatballs. Jason went with the fish and chips.

"So, you'll never believe what I've seen these past three days," Jason blurted out after the server left.

"Try me," Catalina fired back.

"Okay, you're going to think I'm crazy, but here goes: on the first day, the hill to the east of us, you know the one with the lake on the other side of it?"

Catalina nodded.

"I swear I saw it glowing. Not just from the morning sun, I mean actually glowing. And then pulsating."

Catalina looked up and kept a straight face. Jason continued:

"Then I walked over that hill to see if the lake was really on the other side. And it was. I walked to the water's edge and looked across the water. Shortly thereafter, I swear to you, I saw a cross standing nearly ten feet tall! I couldn't believe my eyes! Then the cross began glowing!"

Catalina squinted a little but kept a straight face throughout the story. He continued: "Okay, then on day two, I saw the hill to the east of us glowing and pulsating again! I felt an urge to walk back to the lake, just like I did the day before. This time, I walked around the lake to the other side. And that's when I saw it again: the cross! It appeared out of nowhere at the water's edge! Then it began glowing again! What I saw next is going to frighten you…"

Jason let his sentence hang in the air for suspense. He could feel the drama building. He then wondered if he should tell her what he saw next. *She might think I'm insane!* The silence was deafening and you could hear a pin drop in the diner.

"You saw Jesus Christ?" Catalina deadpanned.

At that moment, their server returned with their meals. Spaghetti and meatballs for Catalina. Fish and chips for Jason. She continued to stare blankly at him until the server left.

"What? Are you ashamed to say 'Jesus Christ'?" she continued with a deadpan stare.

Jason couldn't believe his ears. There was that word again: ashamed. First the angel, then the Bible passage, and now Catalina! She continued:

"And let me guess, you saw an angel this morning that told you not to be ashamed?"

Jason's eyes grew wide. He blinked several times, while Catalina remained catatonic. She then picked up her fork, twirled some spaghetti around it, sank it into a meatball, and brought it to her mouth. Jason sat in stunned silence.

"Mmm," she moaned. "Good spaghetti!"

Jason's jaw dropped. Then he started laughing. Catalina finally cracked a smile and began laughing as well.

"Let me take you back to the lake after we're done eating. I want to show you something."

Jason nodded in agreement. Still amazed and also relieved that Catalina was tuned in to the same wavelength that he was on.

After they finished their meals, Jason and Catalina returned to the Jeep. They headed north back up the highway to the lake. Jason was a bit apprehensive. He looked over at Catalina. She was placid. Serene. Her serenity brought him serenity and he returned his gaze to the highway ahead. When they got close to the lake, Catalina parked her Jeep to the side of the highway.

"I'll show you an easier way," she said.

Jason assumed she already knew about the barbed wire snapping in two and didn't bring it up. Catalina pulled a flashlight from her glove compartment. It was as if she had planned for this very occasion.

Catalina shone the flashlight in front of them as they came to the barbed wire fence. And there, just wide enough to fit through, was a section of fence not enclosed by barbed wire. A new way. An easier way. They made their way up the hill, down the hill, and came to the water's edge.

"We have to go around to the other side," she insisted.

"Lead the way," Jason replied.

As they moved clockwise around the lake, Jason saw something near the banks on the other side. It looked like a small fire burning on the ground. He looked over at Catalina to see if she noticed it as well.

"Keep moving," she instructed.

Jason looked back to the fire, which was still ablaze on the ground near the water's edge. They were quickly approaching the other side. They were fast approaching the fire that burned wild. Jason and Catalina stopped about twenty feet from the fire. She turned off her flashlight.

Then she looked him in the eyes and took his hand.

"Don't be ashamed," she whispered.

At that moment, the cross appeared! It stood just beyond the fire, illuminated by the dancing flames. They both stared straight ahead. Jason tightened his grip on Catalina's hand ever so slightly. Although the images were intense, Jason felt a strange serenity wash over his entire body.

"Don't be ashamed," Catalina whispered again.

Just then, Jesus Christ appeared on the cross! His body glowed by the light of the fire. The dancing flames illuminated the blood and sweat that covered his body. Jason and Catalina held each other tight and were not ashamed. They stared in rapt awe for several seconds before Jason made an observation.

"He's breathing," Jason whispered. "He's alive."

Catalina continued to look on silently at Christ Jesus crucified on the cross, with the fire below illuminating his body.

Just then, the image began to dissipate into the night air. This time, however, Jason let it go without fretting.

Together, Jason and Catalina had witnessed Jesus crucified on the cross. It was something that they knew they would share forever. An image so glorious, they would boast about it and not be ashamed.

As Catalina pulled into Jason's driveway later that night, she looked over and saw him staring straight ahead. She came to a stop at the end of his driveway and put the Jeep in park.

"Thank you, Catalina," Jason said softly.

"Thank *you*," she whispered back.

Just then, Jason leaned in and kissed her. He brought his lips together gently over her lower lip. He could hear her breathing faster. He continued to kiss Catalina for several more seconds. And then, he pulled away.

Catalina's eyes were still closed for a few moments. She brought her lips together and smiled ever so slightly.

"Goodnight," he whispered.

Jason stepped out of the Jeep and headed back to Morning Glory. Catalina started her engine and returned home.

It was a miraculous night, to be sure. One that Jason and Catalina would remember for the rest of their lives.

Chapter 4

Day four at Morning Glory began in a most excellent way. Jason awoke refreshed and feeling better than he had in… perhaps forever! As he scooped the grounds into the coffee maker, a most excellent idea came to his mind: *a passage from the Bible.*

As the coffee brewed, Jason made his way over to the end table where his Bible had now been made a permanent fixture. He turned to the First Letter of Paul to the Corinthians, chapter 13, verses 12 & 13:

For now we see in a mirror dimly, but then face to face. Now I know in part; then I shall know fully, even as I have been fully known. So now faith, hope, and love abide, these three; but the greatest of these is love.

He then set his Bible down on the end table and returned to the kitchen to fetch his coffee. He sauntered out to the deck, per his morning ritual, and took in the splendor of nature.

It was summer at Morning Glory and Jason was well pleased.

He gazed out at the mountain peak, the highest peak in Arizona. He shifted his focus to the hill, which was closer than the mountain. Beyond that hill there was a lake. It was the sight of many visions. Visions now shared with a friend.

At that moment, Jason saw the yellow Jeep come racing down the dirt road. It pulled into his driveway and out came Catalina. She saw him on the second-story deck and shouted:

"Hey! Can you cook?"

Jason rose from his chair and peered over the rail.

"Yes, yes I can!" he replied.

"Great! Can you cook us dinner tonight? At, say, eight o'clock?"

Jason pondered it over for a moment, tilting his head from side to side in a dramatic way.

"Eight sounds great," he affirmed.

Catalina smiled and hopped back in her Jeep. She then sped off down the dirt road.

A few hours later, Jason spotted two cars coming down the dirt road toward Morning Glory. One was a Dodge Charger and the other was a Dodge Challenger. A black Challenger. Both cars pulled into his driveway. He hurried down the steps on the side of the house and greeted the two men.

"This one's for you," the first man exclaimed. He tossed the keys to the Challenger in Jason's direction.

Jason caught the keys and a wide grin came over his face. The new ride had officially arrived. He then thought of a certain someone he could take for a moonlight drive that evening.

After dinner perhaps?

The men from the dealership then left in the Charger and left Jason with the Challenger. He decided to take it for a spin. *To Rocky's Diner!* Jason revved the engine a few times before putting it in drive. He sped off down the dirt road and turned onto the highway.

As he pulled into the diner's parking lot, he noticed a row of motorcycles. Many of the bikes were sporting flame decals. A few were sporting decals that read 666. The gang of bikers exited the diner as Jason parked his new ride. He strolled to the entrance as they walked to their hogs.

"That's the guy," one of the bikers remarked.

Jason continued walking.

"Keep an eye on your girl!" another shouted in his direction.

Just then, Jason turned around. He fixed his eyes on a portly man in wrap-around sunglasses sporting a black leather vest. Jason let out a small chuckle.

"What'd you say?" Jason asked the portly man.

The portly man looked to his left and right, as if to summon his gang for help. Several of them sneered at Jason. A short man with a thin black mustache stepped forward.

"You better watch your back, homie!" he asserted in a threatening tone. He then lifted his right hand and formed the shape of a gun with his index finger and thumb. He pointed his index finger at Jason and flicked his thumb downward twice.

Jason could feel his heart beat faster. He stared directly into the eyes of the short man who threatened him. For several seconds, the two men stared each other down like mad dogs. Jason panned his eyes from left to right, taking in the whole gang of devilish men. He then turned around and walked to the entrance of the diner.

"That's right!" he heard one of them shout.

Jason ignored them and proceeded into the diner. He was seated at a booth by the front window. His server set a menu down on the table and then looked out the window. The bikers were revving their engines. Some were making threatening hand gestures.

"It's alright," he reassured the young server. "All bark, no bite."

She glanced down at him and let out a nervous laugh.

As the gang sped off one by one, he once again noticed the flame decals. And on a few of the bikes, he noticed a 666 decal. Apparently he was known around town. And it only took four days!

Jason left Rocky's Diner after a light lunch and a cup of coffee. He then made his way into town to do some grocery shopping. For on the menu that evening would be chicken piccata! He bought some chicken tenderloins, capers, lemon sauce, and linguine noodles. A bottle of wine for good measure.

Eight o'clock rolled around soon enough. Catalina pulled into Jason's driveway and noticed something different. There was a black Challenger sitting in the garage.

"You like it?" Jason crowed from the deck above.

"Wow!" Catalina replied. "That is one *sweet* ride."

"Climb up those stairs and meet me in the kitchen. I've made chicken piccata!" Jason exclaimed.

He set two plates on the table and poured two glasses of wine.

"A toast," he announced. "To incredible visions and friendship!"

"Here, here!" Catalina roared.

The pair enjoyed their meal and each other's company. The wine flowed and they shared many laughs. Jason found it a good time to tell Catalina about his encounter with the bikers earlier that day at Rocky's Diner.

"So after I get my new ride delivered," Jason started, "I speed on down the highway and stop at our old haunt, Rocky's Diner!"

Catalina let out a snort. She was getting the giggles from the wine.

"Rocky's!" she shouted. "I love that dumpy little diner!"

She snorted again, which in turn made Jason burst into laughter. Once he caught his breath, he continued:

"It *is* a dumpy diner! You are so right!" Jason agreed. "Anyway, I pulled into the parking lot and there's a whole row of motorcycles taking up, like, fifteen spots. I park my car and walk to the door and then this guy yells, 'Keep an eye on your girl!'"

Catalina's expression went from silly to serious in a split second. She put her glass of wine down on the table.

"Did they have 666 decals on their bikes?" Catalina asked nervously.

"Some of them did, yeah," Jason responded. "Most of them just had those common flame decals."

Catalina looked down. She looked genuinely shaken by the news.

"The ones with the flame decals are relatively harmless," she explained. "But the guys who ride with the 666 gang are from hell. Like, actually, literally, from hell."

This new revelation sobered Jason up in an instant. Catalina continued: "You see, evil moved into this town before you arrived. They want to stop you."

"Stop me from doing *what*?" Jason asked.

"From writing your book," she replied.

"My book? But I don't have the slightest idea for a book."

Catalina lowered her chin and gazed at him with a deadpan expression. Her big eyes locked onto his in a most disapproving way.

"Really?" she began. "Nothing out of the ordinary has happened to you in the last, I don't know, four days or so?"

Then it hit him. The visions. Catalina. The biker gang. It was all part of the plot. The plot he was living. *Whoa.*

"I asked you to make dinner tonight so that I could tell you that we are going to face challenges and threats directly from the devil himself. You see, my grandmother, Maria, sent me to this town to help keep you safe. To inform you of impending danger. To help you understand your role. And most importantly, to help you keep a cool head while you write your book. Our book."

This sudden bombardment of information was almost too much for him. Catalina continued:

"I'm picking up my grandmother, Maria, tomorrow and bringing her back to my house. She would love to meet you. She has so much to tell you."

"Of course," Jason responded. "I'd love to meet her as well."

"My grandma thinks you're a great writer. She's read all your works of fiction. But now, she insists that you start writing your first work of non-fiction. I'll bring her by for dinner tomorrow at eight o'clock. Make something with chorizo."

"Okay, I can do that," Jason said with a smile. "No joy ride tonight, Cat. Too much vino!"

She giggled out loud.

"Did you just call me *Cat?* And did you just say *vino?*"

Jason walked Catalina home that evening. They stood together at her doorstep for a few moments. Then he left her with a kiss on her forehead. As she went inside her house, Jason walked back to Morning Glory.

Tonight was heavy, he thought, *tomorrow night might be even heavier.*

Chapter 5

Jason woke on the fifth morning with a slight headache. He shuffled to the kitchen and made himself a strong cup of coffee.

While it brewed, he went over to his Bible which sat on the end table. He opened to the Gospel according to John and read from chapter 15, verses 18–19:

If the world hates you, know that it has hated me before it hated you. If you were of the world, the world would love you as its own; but because you are not of the world, but I chose you out of the world, therefore the world hates you.

Jason realized that his first work of non-fiction was going to inevitably ruffle some feathers. Secular publishers would surely run and hide from his message.

But he was, after all, raised a Christian. He never lost his faith entirely. Even in his lowest moments, Jason knew the Spirit would guide him to clearer waters. Now, as he saw it, the past five days had taught him to move back to the Father and the Son.

That morning, as he sipped his coffee on the deck, he felt a strong force beckoning him back to the lake. The lake that was over the hill. He wondered what strange vision he might encounter.

As he made his way to the lake, he used the easier route that Catalina had shown him. He made his way up the hill, making sure to enjoy the view at the top, and then back down the hill.

He walked slowly to the water's edge and set his gaze to the other side. Jason expected to see a cross, maybe even Christ Jesus. Then, something drew his eyes downward. He saw his reflection in the water. The water was clean and calm.

As he continued to look down at the water, his reflection vanished. A new reflection appeared in its place. He saw an older woman. She looked Hispanic, with golden skin much like Catalina's. Just then, the reflection spoke:

"God bless you, my son!"

As she said those words, the woman's reflection in the lake began to fade. Jason smiled and waved as her image disappeared and his own returned. After so many visions, he was no longer frightened. Jason raised his head and stared straight ahead for several seconds. He took a few deep breaths and looked to the sky.

"Thank you, God," he said aloud.

Jason then returned to Morning Glory, hopped in his new black Challenger, and sped off to the local grocery store. He was making dinner that evening for two very special people.

As he cruised down the highway, he thought of all the items he needed: chorizo, banana peppers, Spanish rice, tomatoes, and wine. The Challenger purred like a big cat and Jason gave it some more gas. The fresh summer air filled his car. He took another deep breath and consciously savored the moment.

Jason never imagined that he would rediscover his Christian faith. Years as a novelist in L.A. had jaded him. Relationships came and went, never getting too serious. And if they started to, one party would typically pull the plug. And it wasn't just the city, it was Jason's own embrace of the fast culture. He never thought in a million years that he would be rediscovering his faith in Flagstaff, Arizona with the help of a beautiful woman and visions from God. Sailing down the highway in a brand-new Challenger.

He came out of his daydream just as he arrived at the local grocery store in town, Shopper's Club. He drove slowly through the parking lot, looking for a good spot. As he turned his head to the left, he saw two motorcycles parked next to one another. As he kept driving, he noticed decals on the back of both bikes that read 666.

"They're everywhere," Jason said under his breath. He then parked his car and proceeded into Shopper's Club.

As he strolled down the aisles and put the items in his basket, he could sense a strange energy all around him. Of dark forebodings. He turned around quickly, but the aisle was empty.

He continued to pick up the items he needed.

As Jason was checking out, he saw two short men in leather vests heading toward the exit. They were both wearing wrap-around sunglasses. On their vests, Jason could see patches that read 666. They were the ones from hell that Catalina had warned about.

Jason stared coldly and blankly at the two men as they walked out of the store. The bikers laughed and exchanged some words with one another, but Jason couldn't make out what they said.

As he left the store and walked into the parking lot, he saw the bikers coming toward him. They revved their engines and then sped away. Jason continued to give them a cold stare.

❖

Eight o'clock came soon enough and Catalina arrived in her Jeep on time. Jason descended the steps on the side of the house. He was slightly nervous.

As the passenger door of the Jeep swung open, Jason couldn't believe what he saw! It was the same woman who had appeared to him in the lake earlier that morning! Catalina's grandmother, Maria, was the woman in the water! She walked up to Jason and kissed him on the cheek.

"God bless you, my son," Maria whispered.

Jason smiled and blushed.

"Have you two met before?" Catalina asked in a dry tone.

Jason showed both women up the stairs to his kitchen, where the meal awaited. Banana peppers stuffed with chorizo, a side of Spanish rice, and red wine.

Maria loved the food and helped herself to a healthy glass of wine. Catalina poured herself a glass as well.

"Some people think my granddaughter is too young for you," Maria remarked. "But I tell them: Jason is young at heart. He needs a woman that will be able to keep up with his adventurous spirit."

Jason felt as if he had known Maria his whole life. As if they were part of each other's stories, each other's destinies.

"I agree, Maria," Jason replied. "Your granddaughter is a good influence. Truly, she has brought light back into my life."

Maria wiped a tear across her cheek. Catalina smiled.

"He's seen the visions, too, Grandma," Catalina announced.

This brought a smile to her grandma's face.

"Were you frightened when you first saw the cross, Jason?" Maria asked. "When you first saw Christ Jesus on the cross by the lake?"

"I was," Jason admitted. "But then the fear subsided and I was filled with a sense of ease. A weightlessness, almost. It's hard to describe, but I felt at peace."

"Catalina was frightened as well when she first witnessed Jesus on the cross down by the lake," Maria began. "You see, Catalina moved into her home several weeks before you arrived. I took her down to the lake one morning and Christ appeared, crucified on the cross."

Jason looked over at Catalina, who had tears in her eyes.

"But I told her not to be frightened, not to be ashamed," Maria continued. "For Christ died for our sins and rose to heaven. God the Father, through his Son, taught man the ways of righteousness and how to gain the keys to the gates of heaven."

Jason was amazed. He felt the Spirit alive in the room. All his life he somehow knew that the Spirit was real.

Maria then asked Jason to get his Bible from the end table. She asked him to read aloud from the Letter of Paul to the Romans. Chapter 12, verse 2:

Do not be conformed to this world, but be transformed by the renewal of your mind, that by testing you may discern what is the will of God, what is good and acceptable and perfect.

"The forces of evil, the devil himself, will try and prevent you from writing your testimony, Jason," Maria explained. "The visions that you have witnessed must be documented and shared with the world. Catalina and I will vouch for your testimony. We have seen those same visions!"

Jason raised his eyebrows and took a sip of wine.

"I'm here to help you, Jason," Catalina interjected. "Because you are a great writer and have sold many books in the past, you have a platform. But it's true, your secular agent and secular publisher will abandon you."

Jason was suddenly alarmed. His agent and publisher had been with him from the beginning. His agent, David, was the first one to discover his knack for spinning a good yarn. It was David who took Jason's first novel, *Desperate Times in the West*, to All Terrene Books and sold it. All Terrene, in turn, published Jason's novel and the rest, as they say, is history.

"David and All Terrene will *desert* me? How are you so sure?" Jason begged.

"God speaks to me the same way he speaks to you," Maria replied. "And he wants you to know that betrayal can come from those close to you. Those you have known and trusted for years will abandon you when you begin to share your testimony." Jason squinted his eyes.

"I *know* what I've seen," he declared, "and no one will stop me from spreading the truth. Even if some abandon me, I know that God will put faithful people in their place."

Maria and Catalina were stunned. They did not expect Jason to come around so soon, given the intensity of the visions and the repercussions for spreading his testimony.

"Tomorrow, you should begin writing your story," Maria said to Jason.

He took a gulp of red wine and nodded in agreement.

"So have you two kissed yet?" Maria inquired nonchalantly.

Jason choked on his wine. He began coughing and hunched over in his chair. Maria and Catalina smiled.

"Well, there was that one night…" Catalina began in an excited tone.

Maria beamed a big smile in Jason's direction, which caused Jason to smile. The cat was out of the bag.

And with that, the trio concluded their evening. Jason walked Catalina and her grandmother, Maria, out through the garage.

"Nice ride," Maria commented as she walked past the new Challenger.

The three of them walked slowly down the driveway. Catalina then turned and looked at Jason.

"Thank you… for a wonderful evening," she whispered.

Just then, Maria ran to Jason and kissed him on the cheek.

"God bless you, my son!"

Maria turned and walked back to Catalina's house.

"Goodnight," Catalina said softly.

She gave Jason a peck on the lips and walked away.

Tonight was heavy, Jason thought to himself. *Sometimes heavy is good.*

Chapter 6

The sixth day at Morning Glory began with Jason staring up at his ceiling fan. He did not roll out of bed immediately, but stayed supine for several minutes. Although he felt bad for feeling so, Jason was nervous. Today he would begin writing his new book. His first piece of non-fiction. It had been six years since his latest work. Would there be rust?

"Guide me, Lord," Jason announced into the air. "Let's do this together."

With that, Jason rose from his bed and headed to the kitchen. As his coffee brewed, he made his way out to the deck. The air was cool. The stars shone brilliantly. His new home in the country granted him spectacular views of the night-time sky. He had never seen so many stars!

Jason kept his head tilted back and took in the splendor. Crickets could be heard chirping in the distance. A gentle breeze passed over the land.

"I will be patient," Jason whispered.

As the words left his mouth, a shooting star streaked across the sky! Jason smiled from ear-to-ear. The Spirit was alive and all around him.

Jason went back inside to fetch his cup of coffee. As he took his first sip, he glanced at the Bible on the end table.

He took another sip of coffee then set the mug on the end table. He lifted the Bible and selected a reading from the Gospel according to Luke. He turned to chapter 8 and read verses 16–18 aloud:

"No one after lighting a lamp covers it with a jar or puts it under a bed, but puts it on a stand, so that those who enter may see the light. For nothing is hidden that will not be made manifest, nor is anything secret that will not be known and come to light. Take care then how you hear, for to the one who has, more will be given, and from the one who has not, even what he thinks that he has will be taken away."

Jason knew he had to share his story. There was no turning back. His light was his testimony. And his testimony was part of something greater.

Time to dust off the laptop, he thought.

It had been six years. Was the magic still there? Could he still spin a good yarn? Then it hit him: *I'm not spinning a yarn, I'm telling the truth! But… they'll never believe me!*

Jason began to pace back and forth throughout the living area. His mind raced. His heart began beating faster. He thought of all the worst possible outcomes.

"They'll think I'm nuts!" he shouted.

"Who will think you're nuts?" a voice cut in.

"Ah!" Jason shrieked. He jumped higher than he had ever jumped in his entire life! He looked to his left, and there stood Catalina, sporting her trademark deadpan gaze.

"Oh my God! Oh my God! You could have *killed* me!" Jason shouted.

Catalina smiled ever so slightly.

"Don't be so dramatic," she quipped. "So *who* will think you're nuts?" Jason slowly collected his breath.

"You know… *them.* The unbelievers. My testimony is going to rock their worlds. I'm going to be labeled a kook."

"Why do you care what *they* think?" she countered. "Your testimony is for the believers, not the unbelievers."

This bit of wisdom hit Jason like a ton of bricks. He was trying to appeal to the wrong audience. The wrong crowd.

"You're right," he concluded. *"Hey!* How did you get in?"

"The door was open," Catalina responded matter-of-factly.

"Oh," Jason replied. "That makes sense."

"I just want to let you know that I'm driving my grandma back home now. She *really* likes you, Jason. She thinks you're a great writer. But remember, she wants you to start your first work of non-fiction today. Remember?"

"Of course!" Jason asserted. "My testimony. Tell Maria it was a pleasure meeting her."

"You're such a gentleman, Jason Morrison. Where did you learn your manners?"

Jason smirked and pointed to the sky. Catalina smiled and began walking toward the door that led to the deck.

"Wait!" Jason called. "What's your number?"

Catalina stopped just before she reached the door. She paused briefly before turning around in place. "You want my number, Jason Morrison?" she responded coyly.

"Yes," he asserted, "so we can keep in touch."

Catalina grinned from ear-to-ear and gave Jason her phone number. She then made her way out the kitchen door and down the steps. Jason came out onto the deck and watched as Catalina walked back to her house.

As Catalina hopped into her yellow Jeep, Maria came out the front door. She walked toward the vehicle with a spring in her step. Before she opened the passenger door, Maria looked in the direction of Morning Glory. She spotted Jason on the second-story deck and waved enthusiastically. Jason waved back with a smile across his face.

As the Jeep started down the driveway, Catalina honked her horn twice. She sped off down the dirt road just as the sun rose above the horizon.

Jason headed back inside and noticed his laptop sitting on the counter in the kitchen. It was inviting him. It was intimidating him. He walked over slowly and sat down on a stool. Before opening the laptop, he took a deep breath. Jason could feel it in the air. This was the point of no return.

In a quick move, Jason opened his laptop. *Chapter 1,* he typed. Jason went back to the first day at Morning Glory in his mind. Six days prior. *What was the first sign?* he wondered.

The hill! The glowing hill!

Jason replayed the spectacular visions in chronological order. After he saw the hill aglow, Jason recalled being called to the lake. The lake that sits on the far side of the hill. He remembered the barbed wire snapping in two. He remembered standing at the water's edge and witnessing the cross. The following day the cross reappeared, this time supporting the body of Christ Jesus. He remembered the angel in the aspen grove. The one that told him not to be ashamed. He recalled the first time he told another living soul about the visions. It was Catalina.

At Rocky's Diner. They went to the lake that night under the cover of darkness. They witnessed a fire burning wild. They witnessed the cross appear. And they witnessed Christ Jesus crucified on the cross.

Jason inhaled sharply. He closed his eyes and exhaled slowly. The memories were almost too much to bear.

He remembered making dinner for Catalina the fourth night at Morning Glory. She informed him of his mission. His book. His testimony. On the fifth day, he remembered seeing the reflection of the woman in the water. He recalled her words: "God bless you, my son!" He remembered seeing Maria for the first time that same night. She was the woman in the water! He recalled making dinner for both Catalina and Maria. Maria warned him of the evil that was all around him. The bikers with the flame decals. And the bikers who ride with the 666 gang.

The ones from hell.

Jason took his hands off the laptop at that moment. He glanced around the room and realized how utterly silent it was.

He remembered Catalina's prophecy: both his agent and publisher would abandon him.

His testimony would be too much for them to handle.

Jason stood up at that moment and walked to the front window. He set his gaze upon Humphreys Peak.

"God, give me strength," he spoke aloud.

For the next several hours, Jason sat at the counter clacking away at the keys of his laptop. Page after page was filled with the amazing details of his mystical visions. He was on a roll. It felt great. For a moment, he swore he was back in Los Angeles.

The hours continued to fly by as Jason typed away furiously. He was inspired. It felt like old times. As night fell on Morning Glory and the quiet landscape, Jason triumphantly struck the final key with his middle finger.

"There!" he proclaimed. "All caught up!"

In the matter of one day, Jason had documented every mystical vision. As the cursor blinked on the white page, Jason found himself in real time. He was completely present. He wondered what visions awaited him. How his story would end.

Jason strolled over to the front window and noticed a pair of headlights coming down the dirt road. Sure enough, it was the golden beauty in her yellow Jeep! Catalina had arrived home.

She pulled into her driveway and honked twice. Jason smiled. The watcher was being watched.

Jason turned around and headed to the end table. He picked up his phone and sent a text to Catalina:

Welcome home! How was the drive?

Jason set his phone down and paced a bit throughout the room. Then he heard the all-too-familiar sound of an incoming text. Catalina had replied:

Looong. Exhausting. Did you get any work done, Mr. Famous Writer?

Jason chuckled out loud. He reported the good news back to Catalina:

I did! I'm all caught up! I'm now living in the present moment!

He knew this bit of good news would delight her.

I knew you could do it!

Jason smiled as he looked down at his phone. Then a great idea came to him! He quickly typed a message into his phone:

Want to go for a walk tomorrow morning? At the park?

He eagerly awaited her response. He began pacing around the kitchen, then the dining room, and then through the main living area. The suspense was driving him crazy!

Ding! Like a Pavlov dog, Jason raced across the room and grabbed his phone from the counter. Catalina had replied:

I'd love to! See you at dawn, early riser.

Chapter 7

Jason rose on the seventh day accompanied by a feeling of joy. He noticed that he had a bounce in his step on this particular morning. He could sense that he was moving in a positive direction. His life had meaning.

On this particular morning, Jason was truly happy. He lifted his Bible from the end table and turned to the Letter of Paul to the Colossians. He read aloud from chapter 3, verses 1–4:

If then you have been raised with Christ, seek the things that are above, where Christ is, seated at the right hand of God. Set your mind on things that are above, not on things that are on earth. For you have died, and your life is hidden with Christ in God. When Christ who is your life appears, then you also will appear with him in glory.

Jason understood that it was time to put on a new self. If Christ was going to be at the center of his new life, every aspect of his being would have to reflect that—including his writing. For a moment, he wondered if he could sustain such a Christ-focused existence. Could every future piece of writing really be based in faith?

He set his Bible down on the end table. There it was. An endless source of wisdom. An endless source of material from which to draw upon. Jason could go to the well as many times as his heart desired.

Dawn was about to break. Jason smiled in anticipation. He headed out to the deck to catch the last of the night-time stars.

He glanced up at the sky briefly then adjusted his gaze downward in the direction of Catalina's house. The lights were on. The cat was stirring.

Just then, Catalina stepped out of her front door. She was wearing a white tank top, sky blue shorts, and a pair of white athletic shoes.

"Wow!" Jason exclaimed.

Catalina looked in Jason's direction and let out a small laugh. Jason hurried down the steps and greeted Catalina in his driveway. The pair then walked to the park, which was about a mile down the highway.

Once they arrived, Jason and Catalina strolled down the trail at a leisurely pace. The smell of pine permeated the air. A gentle breeze moved the branches above them back and forth. Jason always felt the Spirit alive in nature. The stillness. The tranquility. And the power. Then Catalina broke the silence.

"So my grandma wants to know: are you Catholic?"

"Yes," Jason replied. "Baptized and confirmed in the church."

"Me too!" Catalina squealed.

"To be honest, though, I kind of lost my religion once I went off to university."

Jason wasn't ashamed to admit that his commitment to God had wavered. He kept up his habit of nightly prayer for the first few months at university, but it wasn't long before he gave it up entirely.

"Me too," Catalina replied in a dejected tone.

She looked down at her feet and Jason could feel her sadness.

"It's okay!" he reassured her. "I think many people raised in the church have experienced doubt."

Catalina raised her head and smiled. "Really?"

"Absolutely!" Jason reassured her. "It's the deepest concept there is, and we're asked to run on faith."

Catalina let out a soft laugh.

After walking a few miles among the ponderosa pines, Jason and Catalina arrived at the aspen grove. The sight of Jason's angelic vision.

"This is where I saw the angel," he started. "I was mesmerized. It was out of this world!"

He looked to the spot just off the trail where he saw the angel floating.

Suddenly, at that spot, the ground began to swirl. The green grass began to twist in a clockwise direction. Loose dirt was thrown into the air as the swirling spot grew larger and larger. Jason pulled Catalina back and held her close. The pair stood transfixed.

The swirling patch of grass and dirt then began to sink deep into the earth. A great hole was created in an instant! The swirling ceased. The sound of silence pierced the air. Jason, still holding Catalina close, looked ahead with his mouth agape.

A few seconds passed before Jason loosened his grip on Catalina. Still amazed, to be sure, he made his way over to the hole that had just been created.

"Be careful!" Catalina shouted.

Jason stepped gingerly and stopped about five feet from the edge.

"Oh my God!" Jason exclaimed as he peered down into the hole.

"What? What is it, Jason?"

"It's so deep. And dark. It looks… bottomless!"

Jason continued to inch closer. Catalina stepped carefully toward the edge. Curiosity had gotten the best of. her.

"Oh my God!" she cried. "Why is it so dark?"

Catalina began to sob as she stared into the deep blackness of the hole. Jason could not keep his eyes off it. His reaction, however, was completely different. Instead of tears, Jason began to laugh uncontrollably. With his eyes wide and pupils dilated, he laughed like a fool while staring into the deep blackness.

"It's a bottomless pit!" Jason roared.

He couldn't divert his eyes from the black abyss.

Just then, Catalina gasped and began to run at full speed down the trail. She sprinted through a maze of white aspen trees. Her eyes were wide and her pupils dilated.

Jason broke his gaze several seconds later. He looked around but Catalina was nowhere in sight.

"Catalina?" he shouted. "Catalina!"

There was no response. When he looked back to the hole, it was gone.

Jason snapped out of his stupor and realized he had to find Catalina. *Did she fall into the abyss?* He sprinted down the trail, but there was no sign of Catalina. *Oh no!* Jason returned to the entrance of the park and looked around in every direction in a frenzy.

"Catalina!" he shouted. "Catalina!"

Again, no response. He took off in the direction of Morning Glory and ran alongside the highway, faster than he had ever run before. He came to the dirt road and continued in a full gallop.

From a distance, he could see someone standing in his driveway. It was Catalina! *Thank God!* Jason decelerated and his full-out sprint became a casual jog. He began taking deep breaths and could feel the sweat pouring down his forehead and the sides of his face. He pushed his hair back with his left hand as he approached Catalina. She looked incensed. Both of her hands were on her hips as she stared into Jason's eyes like a mad dog.

"What happened?" Jason began. "What's wrong?"

Catalina's eyes grew wide and her face became flush.

"What *happened?* What's *wrong?"* she growled. "Do you even remember what you said back there?"

Jason was genuinely perplexed. He jogged his memory while Catalina fumed.

"Uh… no," he replied sheepishly.

Catalina did not divert her stare. He wasn't going to be let off the hook. Jason continued to jog his memory.

"Wait! Okay, I do remember saying something. I remember saying, 'It's a bottomless pit!' That's right! I said, 'It's a bottomless pit!'"

Catalina remained incensed.

"After that, Jason. After you said, 'It's a bottomless pit'…"

Jason remained genuinely perplexed. A few seconds passed. The air was still and silence filled the land.

"I give up," Jason began. "What did I say?" Catalina pouted her lips and inhaled sharply.

"As you were staring into that hole, you kept saying, 'Revelation eleven-seven, Revelation eleven-seven…'"

"Revelation eleven-seven?" Jason asked quizzically.

"Yes!" Catalina roared. "You had a crazed look in your eye. Like a madman!"

Revelation eleven-seven? Jason thought to himself. It didn't make sense to him at first, but then it hit him! The Book of Revelation. The Revelation to John.

"The Book of Revelation!" Jason proclaimed. "Chapter eleven. Verse seven." Catalina's facial expression softened slightly. She relaxed her shoulders.

"It's in the Bible?" she asked.

Jason nodded. Then he looked to Morning Glory; to the living area on the second floor.

He thought of his Bible that sat on the end table. He knew what he needed to do next.

Jason walked past Catalina and began up the steps on the side of the house. He stopped just before he reached the door that led to the kitchen.

"Are you coming?" he asked.

Catalina was still standing in the driveway. She slowly walked to the stairs and took gentle steps upward toward Jason.

When she reached the second level, Jason opened the door and walked directly to the end table. He reached down and gently lifted the Bible from the table. He knew that Revelation was the last book of the New Testament and proceeded to flip through the pages until he had just a small sliver of them in his right hand. He flipped slowly through the Letters of Peter, and then through the Letters of John. He stopped at the Letter of Jude, then proceeded to flip one more page. The Book of Revelation.

He quickly turned to the chapter 11. His eyes darted to the beginning of verse 7, which he read aloud:

And when they have finished their testimony, the beast that rises from the bottomless pit will make war on them and conquer them and kill them.

As the last words left his mouth, Catalina let out a gasp. "No!" she cried out.

A chill went down Jason's spine. Those words again: bottomless pit!

Catalina then ran past Jason and opened the kitchen door. She hurried down the steps on the side of Morning Glory and ran all the way back to her house.

Meanwhile, in the main living area, Jason stood frozen in place. The Bible was still in his hands. He gently set it down on the end table.

Later that evening, Jason stepped out onto his deck and pulled up a chair. He sat down facing the mountain and let out a deep sigh. He was still caught in the afterglow of earlier events.

Jason then directed his gaze in the direction of Catalina's house. The lights were on. A feeling of sadness quickly came over him. He genuinely did not remember saying those words.

He sat perplexed.

Several birds flew through the air as dusk descended upon the land. The hill that stood before him was not glowing. It was silent. The mountain that stood beyond the hill was growing dimmer with each passing minute. It stood powerful. Immovable.

In the distance, Jason could hear the slam of a car door. It was the Jeep. It was Catalina.

A few seconds later, the Jeep took off down the driveway and turned onto the dirt road.

Catalina did not honk her horn this time.

Chapter 8

The first week had passed at Morning Glory. Jason woke feeling refreshed. He threw the comforter off his body and sprung out of bed. Despite the previous day's events, he slept well.

He strolled into the kitchen and fixed himself a cup. Then an idea came to his mind: *select a reading from the Old Testament,* he thought. As the coffee brewed, he made his way to the Bible. He opened to the Psalms. He read aloud from Psalm 30, verses 8–10:

To you, O Lord, I cry, and to the Lord I plead for mercy: "What profit is there in my death, if I go down to the pit? Will the dust praise you? Will it tell of your faithfulness? Hear, O Lord, and be merciful to me! O Lord, be my helper!" There it was again: the pit!

Jason yearned to be a faithful servant of the Lord, much like King David. He was offering his life up to the Lord. His testimony had to be shared. Keeping it to himself would not do. It would not benefit the Lord.

"Please do not cast me down to the pit," Jason said aloud. "I am your faithful servant."

He looked up at the wooden planks above him. His eyes followed the 'A' shape to the highest point. He stared intently for a few moments. He could feel the Spirit.

Jason retrieved his coffee and made his way to the deck. He inhaled through his nose and closed his eyes. A symphony of crickets could be heard in the tall grass nearby. The air was still. Jason slowly opened his eyes. He noticed the yellow Jeep was not parked in Catalina's driveway.

"Hmm," he muttered while taking a sip of coffee.

Dawn was fast approaching. Jason could see the orange glow over the horizon. The outline of the great mountain appeared.

Jason then looked over his shoulder. On the counter rested his laptop. He decided to dedicate each morning to his new book. His new adventure. He did not want to forget any pertinent details, lest any pertinent details be forgotten.

Jason rose and headed back inside. He set his mug down on the counter and opened his laptop. *Time to document yesterday's incredible vision. Time to write about… the pit.*

"I *really* can't believe this," he said while letting out a small laugh.

Jason wrote in an inspired state. It felt good to get back in the saddle. He was on a roll. Time flew by as Jason clacked away at the keys. Then, the all-too-familiar sound of an incoming text message penetrated the air.

Jason leaped off his stool and ran toward the sound! His phone was sitting next to the Bible on the end table. He grabbed the phone and looked down at the screen. It was a text message! From David. His agent. Jason let out a deep sigh of disappointment.

Hey buddy! Call me when you have a minute, the text read.

Jason felt a wave of nausea come over him. He knew what he needed to do next. He had to break the news to his agent, David. He needed to let him know about his new book. Jason took a deep breath and dialed David.

"J-Dog!" David shouted. "How is my favorite fiction writer?"

Jason remembered that David was a fellow early riser. David liked his morning shots of espresso and heading to the gym in the dark.

"David," Jason began in a dry tone, "what's happening?"

"Not much, buddy. Well, actually much *is* going down at the moment, I just don't want to bore you with the details. I mean, not that the details are boring, it's just that you're not privy to them. That's all…"

Jason attempted to interject.

"So how's—"

"Oh! That's right!" David butted in. "Somebody told me that you moved to New Mexico or something. Is that true? Are you there, buddy?"

"Yes, I'm here," Jason replied in an exasperated tone. "And it's Arizona, David. Not New Mexico."

"Ohhh! Arizona, that's right!" David shouted. "But why Arizona, dude? Isn't that, like, a retirement community in the desert?"

Jason let out a small laugh. He remembered David's knack for being unintentionally hilarious at times.

"Well, I live in Flagstaff, David," Jason explained. "You might be thinking of Phoenix… or Tucson perhaps."

"Exactly," David replied. "I think I have an uncle in Phoenix. Anyway, it was the weirdest thing. As I was driving to the gym in the dark this morning, I thought about you. I wondered if you had any new ideas for a book. I mean, it has been years, dude. You can't live in the past forever."

The truth hurt but Jason was ready with a counterpunch. Or was he? Was this the time to tell his agent, David, about his latest work of non-fiction?

"You there, buddy?" David asked.

Jason snapped out of his trance and adjusted the phone against the side of his ear.

"Yes, David, I am here. And yes, I am writing a new book!" Jason let the sentence hang in the air. He was proud.

"Great!" David began. "What's it about? You know, those superhero movies are really big these days. Big profit margins! Are you writing a book about superheroes, Jason?" Jason couldn't help but laugh. He didn't want to, he had to.

"No, David, I'm not writing about superheroes. I'm writing about myself. It's non-fiction."

"Whoa!" David shouted. "Your autobiography! That's far out! But dude, you're, like, thirty-six. Are you really calling it quits? Looking into the rear view? Are you in your rocking chair days?"

"No!" Jason bellowed into the phone. He then paused to laugh again. "I'm not writing my autobiography. And I'm not in my rocking chair days. Quite the opposite, in fact. Since moving out here to Flagstaff, I've seen things."

"What kind of things, dude?" David interjected.

"Visions. Visions of the spiritual variety. I've seen a glowing cross. I've seen an angel. I've seen Jesus Christ crucified. Just yesterday I saw—"

"Whoa! Dude! Are you drinking again?" David questioned authoritatively. "Because that is *not* cool. Especially this early."

"I'm not drunk," Jason asserted, "I'm seeing things very clearly now. I even met someone who can—"

"Listen, Jason, I gotta go," David interrupted. "Call me later after you've slept it off."

Jason became enraged. "I'm not drunk!" Jason shouted.

A few seconds passed. No response.

"Hello? Hello? David?" David had left the chat.

"Unbelievable!" Jason bellowed as he tossed his phone on the sofa.

Later that afternoon, Jason went for a run at the nearby park. He did not witness the bottomless pit again, but he did stop at the same spot in the aspen grove. He did stand and stare at the spot for several minutes. But nothing happened this time.

When he returned to Morning Glory, Jason glanced down at his phone, which still lay on the sofa. He picked it up off the cushion and noticed he had a new text… from Catalina!

Hey! Can you order a pizza tonight? I'm bringing someone special over for dinner.

Jason was intrigued. Who could this mystery guest be? He typed his reply into his phone:

I'll make a homemade pizza! You and your guest will be impressed.

Jason set his phone down on the sofa and began to walk away.

Ding! He smirked and turned around in place. Catalina had replied:

Sounds great!

With that, Jason put on his athletic shoes and headed downstairs to the garage where his black Challenger awaited him. He opened the driver's door with a grin that stretched from ear to ear. He revved the engine a few times, threw it in reverse, and then sped off down the dirt road. He began to think of the ingredients for a pizza. Pepperoni? Mushrooms? Black olives?

The possibilities were endless.

As Jason neared town, he noticed a large 'SOLD' sign on the side of the highway. It was on the property of the old saloon. The one that had been vacant for years.

"Someone bought that dump?" Jason inquired aloud. He slowed down slightly and looked to his right. The old saloon stood in a state of disrepair. A dilapidated mess.

"Good luck!" he quipped in a sarcastic tone.

Jason pulled into the parking lot of Shopper's Club and did not notice a single motorcycle. He strolled to the entrance in peace.

Mushroom and green pepper, he thought. *Mushroom and green pepper!*

He proceeded to grab a basket and then went off down the aisles to hunt for the ingredients. Pizza dough, pizza sauce, mozzarella cheese, mushrooms, and green peppers. Jason grabbed some beer as well. Pizza and beer. Catalina and her mystery guest. The excitement was building.

Jason paid for his items, exited the store, and walked back to his Challenger without incident. No motorcycles. No gang members. Just peace.

As he headed back north up the highway, he passed the 'SOLD' sign once again. This time, however, a man with a hunched posture was milling about the sign. As Jason drove by, the man looked in his direction. He was sporting a devilish grin. His eyes were black and soulless. Jason squinted in displeasure.

The Challenger continued north up the highway. Back to Morning Glory. The image of the man flashed before his eyes a few times on the way back. It was unsettling. Jason tried to shake it off, but couldn't.

Later that evening, Jason stood in his kitchen preparing a large pizza with mushrooms and green peppers. He sang a song to himself as he washed down a pint of beer.

"Mystery guest, oh, mystery guest! Who could you be? Oh, mystery guest. Will you be the worst or will you be the best? My… mystery… gueeeest!" Jason sang the final words into his rolling pin.

"Hi Jason!" exclaimed a voice.

"Ah!" he shrieked.

Jason jumped off the ground and turned to his left. There stood Catalina… and Maria!

He gathered his breath and set the rolling pin on the counter.

"Who knew?" Maria began. "Jason Morrison… famous fiction writer *and* singer!"

Jason's face grew red. He chuckled nervously.

"Who wants pizza?" he asked.

Catalina and Maria sat down at the dining room table. Jason brought the fresh pie over and divvyed up the slices.

"Can I have a beer, Jason?" Catalina inquired.

"Me too!" Maria chimed in.

"Absolutely," Jason replied.

Pizza, beer, and two beautiful women. Jason was blessed indeed.

The trio devoured the pizza and shared several pints of beer. Laughter and great conversation filled the air.

"So Jason," Maria started, "Catalina tells me that you both witnessed a great vision the other day. A scary vision."

"Yes," Jason confirmed. "We went to the nearby park and saw what I can only describe as a bottomless pit. I was mesmerized. I couldn't take my eyes off it. I was laughing like a fool!"

"And Catalina was sobbing?" Maria questioned.

"Yes," Jason confirmed. "Catalina reacted quite differently."

"She said you said something cryptic. Do you remember?" Maria prodded.

"Well… I don't remember saying it, but she says I said 'Revelation eleven-seven. Revelation eleven-seven.' I guess I had a crazed look in my eye. Like a madman."

Maria turned to Catalina and nodded.

"Please get your Bible and read verses 7–13, Jason," Maria implored. "There's more to the passage."

Jason raised his eyebrows and walked over to the end table where his Bible sat. He flipped to the back pages until he reached Revelation. He slowly turned the pages to chapter 11.

He then cleared his throat and read versus 7–13 aloud:

And when they have finished their testimony, the beast that rises from the bottomless pit will make war on them and conquer them and kill them, and their bodies will lie in the street of the great city that symbolically is called Sodom and Egypt, where their Lord was crucified. For three and a half days some from the peoples and tribes and languages and nations will gaze at their dead bodies and refuse to let them be placed in a tomb, and those who dwell on the earth will rejoice over them and make merry and exchange presents, because these two prophets had been a torment to those who dwell on the earth. But after the three and a half days a breath of life from God entered them, and they stood up on their feet, and great fear fell on those who saw them. Then they heard a loud voice from heaven saying to them, "Come up here!" And they went up to heaven in a cloud, and their enemies watched them. And at that hour there was a great earthquake, and a tenth of the city fell. Seven thousand people were killed in the earthquake, and the rest were terrified and gave glory to the God of heaven.

There was a silence all around them. The trio were left spellbound by the word.

"Thank you, Jason," Maria said softly.

Jason then closed the Bible and returned it to the end table. He looked over at Catalina.

She was looking directly at him and beaming with a radiant smile.

"Excuse me," Maria announced. "I have to use the restroom. Where is the restroom, Jason?"

Jason pointed to the far corner of the living area.

"Over there, *Grandma,*" he replied.

Oops! Jason's face grew red. Maria smiled slightly and shuffled off to the restroom.

As the door to the restroom closed, Jason could feel Catalina grab him by the waist.

"My hero!" she exclaimed.

She looked into his eyes passionately. Something had come over Catalina.

"Kiss me!" she demanded.

Jason acquiesced and pressed his lips onto hers. He could feel her passion palpably and reciprocated with even more passion. He noticed his hands move from her hips to her booty. His hands cupped her perfect bottom and began caressing its perfect shape. Catalina moaned in delight as Jason continued to kiss and caress her.

"Ahem!" a voice cut in.

Catalina jumped and Jason released his grip. Maria stood before them with a smile across her face.

"Ready to go, Catalina?" she asked.

"Yes, Grandma," Catalina responded.

She turned back to Jason.

"Bye Jason. Thanks for a *wonderful* evening."

With that, Catalina gave Jason a wink and proceeded to the door that led to the deck.

Jason gazed in rapt awe at Catalina's booty as she strutted to the door. A few seconds later, Maria passed and wagged her finger in his direction. Jason smiled.

Chapter 9

Jason woke to the sound of crickets outside his bedroom window. He smiled and drew the comforter close to his chin. He lay supine for several minutes before finally kicking the comforter off his body. Jason then headed to the kitchen. He was in a good mood. Things were about to happen.

Before he made his coffee, before he read from the Bible, Jason walked out the kitchen door onto the deck. He proceeded down the stairs and walked into the tall grass. The sound of crickets was all around him. Jason then dropped to his knees in the tall grass. He looked skyward and began to speak:

"God, I am your instrument. I am here to serve you. Through your Son, Jesus Christ, teach me all that I need to know. Give me strength."

Jason kept his gaze fixed on the sky above. Then he rose from the grass and headed back to Morning Glory. He walked slowly up the stairs and opened the kitchen door. He walked directly to the Bible. He decided to select another passage from the Psalms. This morning he read Psalm 34, verses 15–22:

Righteous. Jason liked that word. He spoke of righteousness long before he came to Morning Glory. It was one of the core principles of his faith. In fact, someone once asked him what it meant to live as a Christian.

"Default on righteousness," he replied.

The way Jason figured it, we all sin and we will all continue to sin. Christ Jesus was the only one among us free from sin. So we live by his example. We fall short, but we ask Christ for forgiveness. We ask him to correct our wrong-headed ways. We default on righteousness. If we do that, we are living as Christians.

Jason set his Bible down and looked to the highest point in the room, where the planks of wood came together and formed the 'A' shape. He looked intently at the highest point. He gave thanks.

After his morning dose of caffeine, Jason laced up his athletic shoes and headed to the nearby park on foot. He needed to break a sweat. He wanted to exercise his body.

Then he wondered, *Am I going to the park in hopes of seeing the bottomless pit?*

Jason shook the thought from his head as he ran down the trail. The park was empty.

Not another soul in sight. Perhaps that's what attracted him to this park? His meditations with God were undisturbed.

As he continued to run down the trail, he could feel beads of sweat on his forehead. He wiped them away with his left hand. He took long, slow breaths and glanced up at the pine branches swaying in the wind. He inhaled sharply and closed his eyes. The familiar scent of pine filled his nostrils.

When he came upon the aspen grove, Jason slowed his pace. He came to a stop at the spot where the pit had appeared. He waited with bated breath for something to happen. He stared at the spot where the grass and dirt twisted and spiraled around, much like a hurricane.

But nothing happened. Jason felt bad for trying to force a vision. He felt ashamed. *Why do I want to see the pit again?* he thought. *Why am I intrigued by the darkness?*

Jason snapped out of his trance and started running again. Through the aspen grove and back to the park entrance. Down the highway, down the dirt road, and back to Morning Glory.

He hopped in the shower and made himself clean.

After dressing himself in the master bedroom, Jason emerged and walked to his laptop, which sat on the counter in the kitchen. He was sticking to his morning ritual, documenting all events exactly as they occurred. A living, breathing journal, if you will. He then wondered what vision he might see next. *What if they cease altogether?* he thought. This notion made Jason's heart beat faster. He could feel his palms become damp.

Ding! The sound of an incoming text. Jason quickly retrieved his phone. It was a new text… from David.

Hey buddy, hope you're feeling better today. Give me a call when you got a sec.

Jason smirked and threw the phone onto the sofa, where it gently bounced on the cushion. Jason decided to complete his morning ritual first. He opened his laptop and let the words pour onto the page. The volume of his testimony was building. Jason was well pleased.

Once complete, Jason folded his laptop shut and headed out to the deck. The morning sun rose over the mountain's right shoulder and bathed it in sunlight. A most glorious sight indeed.

As Jason continued to stare at the mountain, he felt as if he was being watched. He turned his gaze downward in the direction of Catalina's house. Sure enough, the cat was stirring. Catalina was strutting down her driveway and looking directly at Jason. A wide smile was across her face. Jason smiled back and waved. Catalina turned her head quickly as she neared the Jeep. Her ponytail hung in mid-air. Oh, senorita!

Just then, Maria stepped out the front door and began to walk toward the Jeep. As she approached the passenger door, she spotted Jason on the second-story deck. Maria waved and beamed a great smile. Jason waved back.

As the Jeep pulled out of the driveway, Jason knew what he had to do next. He had to check in with his agent. He went inside, picked up his phone, and dialed David.

"J-Dog!" David shouted. "Feeling better, my man?" Jason had to consciously pause and center himself.

"Yes, David!" he said in a sardonic tone. "I feel *great!*"

"Wonderful, wonderful!" David began. "I'm willing to forget about that little episode you had yesterday and just blame it on the alcohol. You know, Jas—"

"I wasn't drunk, David," Jason asserted calmly. "Everything I said was the truth. I *have* been seeing things. Great things. I've met a girl. She's seen the visions as well. There's no denying that something special is going on here."

Jason let the words hang in the air. There was silence on the other line. The seconds felt like minutes as Jason awaited David's response.

"You're *serious?*" David asked.

"Yes," Jason replied matter-of-factly.

"Are you *super* serious?"

Jason could then hear David cracking himself up. David guffawed into the phone and all Jason could do was grin and wait for his laughter to subside. Jason rolled his eyes.

"Yes, I'm *super* serious," Jason replied. "No joke. I'm not pulling your leg or yanking your chain. I've already documented all the events that have happened so far. Each morning I make a new entry."

"Like a journal!" David shouted. "So this is non-fiction, dude?"

"Yes, everything I am writing down in my new book actually, literally happened. To me. And Catalina."

"Whoa! Hang on there, buddy! You never told me there was a chick! You *dog!"*

Jason couldn't help but crack up. David continued:

"Tell you what… you send me a copy of that manuscript. Send me what you have so far. I'll give it the once-over and we'll go from there. Sound good, buddy?" Jason rolled his eyes.

"Sounds *great,"* he replied. "I'll send my manuscript over as soon as possible."

"Aces, dude!" David exclaimed. "No guarantees that I'll like it, though. I mean, it sounds far-fetched."

Jason let out a small laugh.

"No problem. Just give it the once-over. I think it has lots of potential."

With that, David left the chat. Jason set his phone down gently on the end table and decided to make some time for himself.

He strolled downstairs and turned into the guest bedroom. In the corner stood a dresser. Jason sauntered over and pulled the top drawer open. Inside, there rested a glass jar. He twisted the top of the glass jar open and brought it to his nostrils.

"Ah!" he exclaimed.

It was the all-too-familiar smell of marijuana. Herb. Ganja. Weed.

Jason had not enjoyed a smoke since moving to Morning Glory. That was about to change. He grabbed rolling papers and a lighter from the top drawer and began to roll a joint. He licked the adhesive strip on the paper and folded it over tightly. *Where should I smoke this?* he contemplated. There was a small patch of pine trees just behind his house, on the western edge of his property. It was secluded.

Jason, with joint and lighter in hand, walked out of the garage and around to the back of his house. He eyed the small patch of trees from a distance and continued walking. As he got closer to the pines, Jason began to think about the times when he would smoke weed alone at university. Those times were etched in his memory. The solitude, along with the herb, brought Jason into a new world.

Jason made his way into the grove and saw many needles scattered on the ground. They crunched beneath his shoes. He looked for a good place to stop and light his joint. There was a small clearing in the middle of the grove. Sunlight shone down in brilliant rays.

Jason stopped suddenly before he reached the clearing. He felt a strange sensation come over him. It was peaceful but demanded his attention. His eyes moved to the center of the clearing, where the sun's rays were illuminating the grass. His eyes grew wide. His pupils dilated.

Just then, the ground at the center of the clearing began to rumble. Jason could feel small tremors beneath his feet. Suddenly, a large stone rose from the ground! Clumps of dirt and grass were hurled into the air, landing with heavy thumps all around the giant stone! A large smile spread across Jason's face. He was in awe.

The stone rose nearly four feet out of the ground. It was pewter with small white flecks. Jason slowly approached the object. It was slender, like a monument, with a gentle slope at the top. Jason circled the stone and observed its perfect shape.

"It's a podium!" he announced. "A stone podium!"

Jason moved closer to the object. The gentle slope at the top of the stone formed a shelf.

The shelf was waist-high.

"I can set my Bible here," he declared, "and read passages." Jason looked to the sky. Rays of light shone down upon his face.

"Thank you," he said.

Jason rested his joint and lighter on the newly-created stone podium and ran back to Morning Glory. He couldn't wait until the next morning. He had to christen the stone immediately. Jason retrieved his Bible from the end table and quickly ran back to the clearing in the grove of ponderosa pines.

He picked up his joint and lighter from the stone and transferred them to his pocket. Then, he gently laid the Bible upon the natural shelf.

It glowed with a magnificent aura as soon as Jason set it down! He took a few steps back. A brilliant radiance emanated from the book. Jason was in awe.

A strong breeze was kicked up at that moment. The pine branches above began to sway. The pages of the Bible began to flip with the strong gusts. Jason took a few more steps back and continued to look on in amazement.

Suddenly, the Bible stopped glowing. The pages stopped turning. Jason was filled with fear. Nevertheless, he walked toward the stone podium where the Bible lay. He stood over the book and looked down. It was opened to the Gospel according to Matthew. His eyes were drawn to chapter 21. He read verses 42–44 aloud:

Jesus said to them, "Have you never read in the Scriptures: 'The stone that the builders rejected has become the cornerstone; this was the Lord's doing, and it is marvelous in our eyes'?"

"Therefore I tell you, the kingdom of God will be taken away from you and given to a people producing its fruits."

"And the one who falls on this stone will be broken to pieces; and when it falls on anyone, it will crush him."

Jason then took the joint and lighter from his pocket. With a flick of his thumb, he created fire. Jason inhaled deeply and witnessed the red glow at the end of the joint. A thin whisp of smoke rose from the tip. He squinted and continued to inhale. Then he paused and looked around the clearing. It was perfectly silent. Perfectly peaceful.

Jason exhaled a white cloud of smoke into the air. It billowed and rose slowly toward the sky above. He continued to draw from the joint and exhale the white smoke into the air.

Minutes later, he took a final puff.

How do I keep the Bible protected from the elements? he thought. Then an idea came to him. Jason raced back to Morning Glory and entered the garage. In the corner rested a wooden chest, large enough to fit a book and other items. He lifted the chest and gauged its weight. Not too heavy. Just right.

Jason carried the wooden chest back to the clearing in the pine grove. He set it down on the ground to the right of the stone podium. Then he lifted the top of the chest. It was empty.

Perfect!

Jason lifted the Bible from the stone podium and transferred it to the wooden chest. He slowly closed the chest and sprang back to his feet.

A new vision! he thought. *New material!*

Later that evening, Jason brought an ice-cold beer out to his deck. He pulled up a chair and positioned it to the east, facing the mountain. Jason then brought the pint glass to his lips and took a gulp.

As the sun set behind him, Jason looked out over the land. Birds flew in groups as dusk arrived. The tall grass in the meadow below swayed in the breeze. And the mountain stood still.

Powerful.

In the distance, Catalina's Jeep could be seen racing down the dirt road. This brought a smile to Jason's face. She turned into the driveway of the second-to-last house on the right and came to a stop near her front door.

Catalina hopped out of the Jeep and ran to the front door of her house. Jason pouted his lips ever so slightly.

Just then, Jason heard the all-too-familiar sound of an incoming text message from inside his living room. He rose slowly from his chair and took a healthy swig from his pint glass. He entered the living area and gently lifted his phone from the end table. It was a text from Catalina!

Hey! Hope your book is going well. I had a great time last night. Grandma did too.

Sleep well, handsome author!

Jason smiled from ear-to-ear and replied to Catalina:

Hi! The book is going great! I had a great time last night as well. You're such a good kisser!

A few seconds passed. *Ding!*

Catalina sent Jason a smiling emoji, which made him smile.

Chapter 10

The tenth day at Morning Glory began with Jason waking from a nightmare. He dreamed that he was standing on his deck, like he does every morning. In his dream, he heard a plane coming from behind him. Jason ran around the deck, to the western side. Sure enough, a plane was flying through the air and descending lower and lower with each passing second. Jason ducked as the plane flew dangerously close over Morning Glory.

Jason then ran around to the other side of the deck. To the eastern side, which faced the mountain. The plane continued barreling eastward at a dangerously low altitude. Jason was held frozen in place on his deck. He tried to yell, but no sound came out. The plane hurdled through the air at several hundred miles per hour. It was a commercial jet. *There could be innocent passengers onboard!* As the plane grew increasingly closer to the side of the mountain, Jason attempted to scream once again. But once again, no sound came from his mouth.

Boom! The jumbo jet crashed into the mountain. A great fireball rose from the impact site. Jason's eyes grew wide. Tears began to well up.

The crash created a great fire that began to burn wild across the side of the mountain. It quickly spread and engulfed every tree in its path. Jason looked on helplessly in absolute terror.

The fire consumed more and more acreage with each passing moment. Jason's heart beat faster and faster. He felt as if he was going to die. And then…

He woke. His heart was still beating fast and he looked up wide-eyed at the ceiling fan.

Jason took a deep breath and exhaled fully. He was relieved it was just a dream.

Jason slid off the side of his bed and walked slowly into the kitchen. He turned on the coffee maker, scooped some grounds, and started the brewing process. The machine hummed as Jason made his way to the deck. He walked down the stairs and around to the back of his house. Darkness was all around, but the moonlight guided Jason on this particular morning. He continued to the pine grove. As he came upon the tall trees, he lifted his head gently and looked up at the moon. It was a glorious sight. The moon was glowing in the sky with silhouetted pine trees rising to the heavens.

Jason walked to the clearing and smiled as he came upon the stone podium and wooden chest. He bent down, opened the chest, and looked inside. Jason noticed something resting atop the Bible. It was a headlamp!

Jason looked to his left, and then to his right. No one was around. The air was still and the sound of crickets grew louder.

Jason then gently scooped the headlamp by its strap from the wooden chest. He pressed a button on top of the headlamp. It emitted an artificial glow. Jason then fit the strap around the top of his head, with the lamp facing forward. He adjusted the lamp so it shone downward on the Bible. *Awesome!* Jason was now able to read Bible passages at any hour. He looked to the sky.

"Thank you," he said with gratitude.

On this morning, Jason decided to read from the Second Letter of Paul to the Thessalonians. He turned to chapter 1 and read verses 5–12 aloud:

This is evidence of the righteous judgement of God, that you may be considered worthy of the kingdom of God, for which you are also suffering—since indeed God considers it just to repay with affliction those who afflict you, and to grant relief to you who are afflicted as well as to us, when the Lord Jesus is revealed from heaven with his mighty angels in flaming fire, inflicting vengeance on those who do not know God and on those who do not obey the Gospel of our Lord Jesus.

They will suffer the punishment of eternal destruction, away from the presence of the Lord and from the glory of his might, when he comes on that day to be glorified in his saints, and to be marveled at among all those who have believed, because our testimony to you was believed. To this end, we always pray for you, that our God may make you worthy of his calling and may fulfill every resolve for good and every work of faith by his power, so that the name of our Lord Jesus may be glorified in you, and you in him, according to the grace of our God and the Lord Jesus Christ.

Jason loved reading from the Letters of Paul. The story of Paul fascinated him. How he was once a strict Pharisee who persecuted the early followers of the Way. Paul even oversaw the stoning of St. Stephen. Despite all this, God looked favorably upon Paul. He revealed the power of truth through his son Jesus Christ as Paul headed down the road to Damascus.

If the Lord can redeem a sinner like Paul, Jason thought, *then surely he can offer the same forgiveness to me.*

"I am yours, God," Jason spoke into the night air. "I am your vehicle. Show me the way."

With that, Jason returned his Bible and headlamp to the wooden chest. He closed the top as a feeling of happiness washed over him. He headed back to his house to fetch his morning cup of jo.

Per his new morning ritual, Jason opened his laptop and wrote about the incredible events of the prior day. He was still filled with a feeling of happiness as he pounded away at the keys.

Then he remembered something. David… the manuscript. Jason let out a deep sigh and continued typing. Once he completed his retelling of the previous day's events, Jason composed a new email and attached the manuscript. He quickly sent it off to his agent.

"Hope you enjoy!" Jason remarked sardonically.

Whether David *liked it* or not made no difference. Jason decided at that moment to complete his testimony, no matter what.

At sunrise, Jason looked to the mountain. It was perfectly intact. No evidence of a plane crash or raging wildfire. He let out a sigh of relief. Then Jason looked down toward Catalina's house. The yellow Jeep was parked in the driveway. He saw her come out her front door at that moment. The cat was stirring.

Jason waved enthusiastically from the deck above. Catalina waved back. She walked down the length of her driveway and turned toward Morning Glory. A feeling of euphoria came over Jason. She walked up Jason's driveway and came to a stop just below the deck.

"You'll never guess who bought that old saloon," she started.

Jason looked from side to side, perplexed.

"I give up… who?" he asked.

"The 666 gang!" she exclaimed. "The guys from hell! The 'grand' reopening is tomorrow."

Jason rolled his eyes and sighed.

"Seriously?" he began. "They bought a *saloon?"*

Catalina let out a laugh.

"Yep… they bought a *salooooon."*

Jason burst into laughter.

"Wanna come up?" he asked confidently. "I've finished my writing. I'm kind of bored." Catalina smiled slightly.

"Sure," she said. "I'm kind of bored, too."

With that, she hurried up the stairs and made her way into the kitchen. Jason's laptop was closed and sat on the counter. Next to it sat a glass jar.

"What's *that?"* Catalina asked inquisitively, pointing to the glass jar.

"What's *what?"* Jason responded innocently.

"That!" she cried, while pointing to the glass jar.

"Oh, *that!"* Jason began. "That's marijuana. Herb. Ganja. Weed."

Silence filled the room. Catalina sported a deadpan gaze. Jason smiled in an attempt to bring down her defenses. He held the smile for what felt like minutes.

"Oh!" she replied. "I've heard of that."

Jason rolled his eyes and took a deep breath in. He exhaled into the air and let out a small laugh.

"You've *heard* of it? *Really?* You've *heard* of it?"

"Yeah," she responded. "I think I tried it once."

Jason opened his mouth and raised both of his hands in exasperation.

"Seriously? You *think* you tried it once?"

Catalina continued to sport a deadpan gaze. Silence filled the room once again. Then, the pair burst into laughter at the same time.

"Okay… okay… I *did* try it once. But I didn't get high," she confessed.

Jason smiled.

"You probably got subpar stuff. Schwag, most likely." Catalina sighed.

"Yeah. It was with my ex-boyfriend. We ended up arguing the whole night." Jason pursed his lips and changed the subject quickly.

"Wanna try again?" he cajoled. "I bet you'll get high this time."

Catalina blushed. She looked down at the floor and inhaled deeply.

"Well," she began, "okay. Just a couple puffs." Jason smiled contentedly.

"I'll show you a secret spot. You'll never believe this, but…" Jason stopped. "Okay, actually you *will* believe this… a large stone rose from the ground behind my house just yesterday. In front of my very eyes. It's shaped exactly like a podium, with a shelf and everything. A stone podium!"

Catalina looked impressed.

"Wow," she said. "This really *is* happening, isn't it?"

Jason chuckled and began to roll a joint. The pair then headed to the clearing in the middle of the pine grove. And there, just as Jason had promised, stood the stone podium.

"Wow," Catalina whispered. "It's beautiful. What's in the wooden chest?"

Jason bent down and opened the chest. He pulled out his Bible and placed it on the stone.

On the shelf.

"Read a passage!" she squealed. "I like hearing your deep voice."

Jason blushed and opened to the Song of Solomon. He read from chapter 8, verses 1–4:

Oh that you were like a brother to me who nursed at my mother's breasts! If I found you outside, I would kiss you, and none would despise me. I would lead you and bring you into the house of my mother—she who used to teach me. I would give you spiced wine to drink, the juice of my pomegranate. His left hand is under my head, and his right hand embraces me! I adjure you, O daughters of Jerusalem, that you not stir up or awaken love until it pleases.

"I liked that one!" Catalina declared.

Jason reached into his pocket and pulled out the joint and lighter.

"Can Christians smoke herb, Jason?" she asked.

"I think so," Jason said. "I mean, Jesus' first miracle *was* turning water into wine."

"*Really?*" Catalina asked quizzically.

"Yep!" Jason responded confidently. "So, I think he liked to party. And he *was* the main dude in Christianity. So..." Jason paused for effect. "Watch this..."

Jason flicked the lighter and fire appeared. He guided the flame to the end of the joint and took a deep drag. He held the smoke for several seconds and then exhaled a white cloud into the air above. Jason took a second puff and then passed the burning joint to Catalina.

She took a delicate drag and held it for a couple seconds. She then exhaled a thin whisp of smoke into the air and passed the joint back to Jason.

"I woke out of a nightmare this morning," Jason said as he took a puff. "I dreamed that an airplane flew over Morning Glory and then crashed into Humphreys Peak. When it hit the side of the mountain, I heard a tremendous boom! And then a great fireball appeared!"

Catalina looked straight ahead, squinting her eyes. Jason took another puff and continued:

"The fire from the crash spread to the trees on the side of the mountain. It created a wildfire that burned uncontrollably across the mountainside. My heart started beating faster and faster. And then... I woke."

Catalina looked into Jason's eyes.

"What do you think it means?" she asked.

"I'm not sure yet," he replied.

Jason took a few more puffs before flicking the joint into the surrounding grass. Jason and Catalina continued talking in the middle of the clearing, seated on the ground next to the stone. They enjoyed each other's company. Jason felt at peace.

"I feel sleepy," Catalina announced. "I'm going to take a nap."

The pair rose to their feet and Jason returned the Bible to the wooden chest. He gently closed the top and walked back with Catalina.

"See you later," Jason said as they came to his driveway.

"See you later," Catalina replied as she headed back to her house.

Jason proceeded up the stairs on the side of Morning Glory and entered through the kitchen door. He made a bee line to the sofa and lay on his back while staring at the highest point in the room. Where the planks formed the 'A' shape. His eyelids grew heavy. Soon, sleep overtook him.

Jason woke a few hours later to a tapping sound. Catalina stood outside on the deck with a smile on her face. He rose from the sofa and slowly made his way to the door.

"Hey!" Catalina said. "Did you take a nap, too?" Jason rubbed his eyes and smiled.

"Yeah. I needed that."

"I was thinking we could go to the park," she said in a bright and bouncy tone. "I have lots of energy to burn now!"

Jason acquiesced and threw on a pair of athletic shoes. The duo walked down the dirt road and along the side of the highway to the park.

As they started down the trail, Jason glanced at Catalina from the corner of his eye. *Is she hoping to see something?* he wondered. Catalina looked at Jason and smiled.

The pair walked for miles in peace. The summer air was filled with the scent of pine. Golden needles could be felt beneath their feet. Then they came to the aspen grove. Jason looked at Catalina to see if she was alright. She looked placid. Serene.

They passed the spot where Jason had first witnessed the angel. The spot where they both saw the bottomless pit. Jason looked at Catalina as they passed the spot. She was looking straight ahead. They walked through the grove and came upon an open meadow. Catalina spotted something in the distance.

"Look!" she cried. "It's a pig!"

Catalina enthusiastically pointed toward the meadow. Sure enough, a hairy little pig was running through the tall grass. And then, three more pigs emerged from the grass, running behind the first pig.

"Javelina!" Jason bellowed. "A pack of peccaries!"

"A pack of *what?*" Catalina asked.

"Javelina. Those hairy little pigs are called javelina, or peccaries." Catalina squealed with delight.

"I want one!"

The pair moved close, but not too close, to the pack of peccaries. Jason and Catalina looked on and were fascinated by the small family of hairy pigs.

"They're so *cute!*" Catalina exclaimed gleefully. "Can we take one back with us? It can live with you at your house. It can be your new companion! I'll come over and feed it twice a day, and you can take it for walks!"

Jason shot Catalina a serious look.

"I already have a hairy little pig," he quipped as he began tickling her tummy.

Catalina squealed and pulled away. She ran closer to the peccaries and began to wave in their direction.

"Come on," Jason implored, "let's keep walking."

They walked the remainder of the trail and returned to the entrance of the park. They walked together along the side of the highway, along the dirt road, and back to Morning Glory.

The pair came to a stop as they neared the garage.

"You still haven't taken me for a ride," Catalina began, "in your new Challenger." She pointed to the black muscle car that sat in the garage.

"You're right!" Jason replied. "How about tomorrow? I'll drive us to that dumpy old saloon. For their 'grand' reopening!"

Jason formed air quotes with his fingers. Catalina laughed out loud, then became serious.

"Wait," she said sharply, "you actually want to give the 666 gang business?" Jason smirked.

"Keep your friends close and your enemies closer," he answered.

Just then, Catalina inched closer to Jason. He smiled and put his hands on her hips. The pair locked eyes and Jason began to kiss Catalina.

It began slow and sensual, then gradually built to deep, passionate kissing. Catalina moaned and breathed heavily. Jason's hands once again found themselves on her perfect bottom and began to gently caress its shape. He squeezed her booty gently. She moaned and exhaled through her nose. Then, she pulled away.

"Let's take it slow," she whispered softly. "We shouldn't stir up or awaken love until it pleases."

Jason quickly remembered the Bible passage he read earlier at the stone podium, from the Song of Solomon.

"Right," he agreed. "Until it pleases…"

Catalina then gave Jason a peck on the lips and turned in place. She strutted with confidence down his driveway. Jason couldn't help but gaze at her booty.

Until it pleases, he reminded himself.

Chapter 11

The ceiling fan spun and buffeted the air around the master bedroom. Jason's eyes slowly opened. The familiar sound of crickets could be heard just outside his window. Fresh air poured in. It smelled sweet.

Jason sprung out of bed. He now had a new morning routine to adhere to: read Bible passage on stone podium as coffee brews, continue writing book while sipping java, brush teeth, get clean in shower, and see what adventure the day brings!

The coffee began to brew as Jason made his way outside. Once again, the moonlight provided visibility. It guided him to the stone podium, which sat in the clearing of the pine grove. He bent down low and opened the chest. Jason retrieved both the Bible *and* the headlamp. He laid the Bible upon the stone podium and adjusted the light that shone from atop his head. He moved it downward until it illuminated the pages.

Jason opened to the Gospel according to Mark and read from chapter 3, verses 21–30:

And the scribes who came down from Jerusalem were saying, "He is possessed by Beelzebul," and "by the prince of demons he casts out the demons." And he called them to him and said to them in parables, "How can Satan cast out Satan? If a kingdom is divided against itself, that kingdom cannot stand. And if a house is divided against itself, that house will not be able to stand. And if Satan has risen up against himself and is divided, he cannot stand, but is coming to an end. But no one can enter a strong man's house and plunder his goods, unless he first binds the strong man. Then indeed he may plunder his house."

"Truly, I say to you, all sins will be forgiven the children of man, and whatever blasphemies they utter, but whoever blasphemes against the Holy Spirit never has forgiveness, but is guilty of an eternal sin"—for they were saying, "He has an unclean spirit."

Jason was impacted deeply by this particular passage. He recognized scribes in his own life. From childhood to the present day. Those people who put on pleasant appearances in public and made sure to say the right things. They were, however, more than willing to turn over the righteous ones when it suited them.

No matter! he thought to himself. *As long as I follow the path of righteousness, I will be with God.*

Jason closed the Bible and returned it to the wooden chest. He turned off his headlamp and set it in the chest next to the Bible. Then he stood up and placed both his hands on the stone podium. It was cold. Powerful.

Jason returned to the kitchen and fetched his cup of coffee in one hand and lifted his laptop with the other. He decided to write on the deck this morning, as the sun rose over the right shoulder of Humphreys Peak.

❖

When the afternoon arrived, Jason found himself on the deck once again. It was a beautiful day. With an elevated view, he continued to observe the wonders of nature. Then he spotted Catalina emerging from her abode. She walked up his driveway and peeked in his garage.

"I'm ready!" she announced. "Take me for a ride in your muscle car, Jason!"

Jason cracked a smile and made his way down the steps. He turned into the garage and opened the driver's door. He sank into the seat as Catalina sank into hers.

"Wow!" she said. "It still has that new car smell!"

Jason started the engine and revved it a few times. He backed out of the garage then sped off in a flash. He accelerated down the dirt road and turned onto the highway. The pair then headed south into the heart of town. To the old saloon.

"So tell me again," Jason said while cruising down the highway, "what's the difference between the common bikers and the ones who ride with the 666 gang?"

"Well, they're all part of the same gang, if you will," Catalina began to explain. "They all ride motorcycles and they all wear black leather vests. And they're all evil." Jason nodded. Catalina continued:

"But only the ones from hell are allowed to put the 666 decals on their bikes. And only the ones from hell are allowed to sew the 666 patches onto their black leather vests."

"What about the other guys?" Jason inquired.

"The other guys are *not* from hell," Catalina began. "But they're still evil. They're not allowed to put 666 decals on their bikes, only those common flame decals. And they're not allowed to sew the 666 patches onto their vests."

"So what's in it for the common guys? The ones with the common flame decals on their bikes? And bare vests?" Jason asked in earnest.

"They're stooges, dude," Catalina replied. "Dupes. Patsies. Fall guys."

"Ohhh," Jason acknowledged.

"The 666 guys hold the chance of membership out like a carrot on a stick. They tell the commoners that they *might* be able to join the 666 gang if they're *really* evil. But no matter what the commoners do, they'll never be able to join the 666. Not *really*. They're not from hell!" Jason pouted his lips.

"Hmm," he muttered as he gave the car some gas.

The black Challenger zoomed down the highway and the duo made their way into town.

As they approached the old saloon, they noticed the 'SOLD' sign had been removed from the property. Jason turned right into the parking lot.

A giant white banner was stretched across the doorway. 'GRAND REOPENING' it read in red letters. A row of fifteen motorcycles were parked near the entrance. Jason counted six bikes sporting the 666 decals.

Jason and Catalina stepped out of the Challenger and walked slowly to the entrance of the old saloon. They continued through the front door and onto the beer-soaked floor. Jason quickly gathered that no renovations were made before the 'grand' reopening. He took a few sticky steps toward the bar with Catalina by his side.

"It stinks in here," Catalina remarked to Jason.

A few of the bikers seated at the bar turned and scowled.

Jason then looked behind the bar and noticed a man with a hunched posture. As the man turned around, Jason recognized him immediately. It was the same man who was milling about the 'SOLD' sign the other day. He was sporting the same devilish grin. His hair was gray and hung in wispy threads. His eyes were dark and bulged out of his head.

"What'll it be?" the barkeeper barked.

Jason and Catalina looked at one another.

"I'll have a Coke," Jason answered.

"Me too," Catalina said hesitantly.

With that, the barkeeper grunted and fetched the colas.

"What kind of a man goes to a bar and doesn't drink?" a short biker with a scar across his left cheek asked. The rest of the gang sneered and laughed in unison.

"I'm the driver," Jason replied. "The designated driver."

His words left the room quiet. The bikers looked around at one another. Then, a biker with a gold tooth chimed in.

"More like designated *sissy!*" the biker roared.

Another wave of laughter rolled through the room. Jason rolled his eyes. Just then, the barkeeper returned with their Cokes.

"That'll be six dollars," the barkeep bellowed, "and sixty-six cents."

As the words left his mouth, he flashed his signature devilish grin. Jason threw a ten-dollar bill on the counter.

"Keep the change," he asserted.

The barkeeper grabbed the bill off the counter and grunted.

Just then, a short man emerged from the back room. He was sporting a black leather vest with a 666 patch sewn onto the left breast. He walked slowly through the bar with a ghastly snarl on his weather-beaten face. Catalina tapped Jason on the shoulder and whispered into his ear.

"That's the leader of the 666 gang. His name is Bill Banner."

The short man continued to walk through the room at a slow pace. The other bikers looked in his direction and nodded.

Bill had short gray hair. Buzzed very close to his scalp. As he walked closer, Jason noticed it was a flat top! Bill's face was adorned with glasses. Large Coke-bottle glasses that made his eyes look like he was peering through a fishbowl. Jason tried his best not to laugh as Bill sauntered over.

"Well!" Bill shouted so the entire room could hear. "Ain't you the writer from New York City?"

"New York *City?*" a biker wailed from across the room.

"No," Jason corrected, "I just moved here from Los Angeles."

"Los Angle-eeze!" Bill shouted loudly. "I bet there were plenty of pretty girls just like *her* back in Los Angle-eeze!"

Bill shifted his gaze to Catalina, who stood to Jason's left, sipping her Coke.

"Not really," Jason replied matter-of-factly. "Not as beautiful as Catalina."

Catalina blushed.

"Catalina!" Bill shouted. "You live on that dirt road, 'bout twenty miles north up the highway. Next to Jesus boy here!"

Jason took a few steps toward Bill and looked him dead in the eye.

"You're not going to do anything… *old* man!"

Several of Bill's men came to his aide. Jason noticed that some of them were packing heat.

"It's okay, boys," Bill began. "It's only a matter of time before we run these Jesus freaks out of town."

"You shouldn't have said that, Bill. Very, very bad," Jason stated calmly while looking the old man in the eye.

"Let's go, Jason," Catalina implored as she pulled him toward the door.

"That's right!" Bill howled. "Take yer broad and get out!"

Jason twisted his upper body around as he walked toward the door. He raised his right index finger and wagged it in Bill's direction.

Jason and Catalina exited the bar and walked back to the Challenger. A few bikers came out and started milling around the entrance, making threatening hand gestures. Jason revved his engine and drove out of the parking lot, back to the highway.

As they arrived back at Morning Glory, Jason could sense Catalina's unease. He pulled into the garage and turned the engine off.

"Well, that's my first and last time at the old saloon," Jason said.

Catalina let out a nervous laugh.

"Yeah. The whole place had a strange vibe," she said.

Jason sighed and looked straight ahead.

"So… I counted six bikes with the 666 decals. Fifteen bikes total. If my math is correct, and I think it is, that means there are nine flunkies."

Catalina smiled.

"Yep. There are six from hell and nine pissants," she confirmed.

"Wanna come upstairs?" Jason asked. "Watch some TV? Make some nachos?"

"Sorry, I can't," Catalina replied. "I'm picking up my friend, Alma, from the airport tonight. She's going to stay at my place for a few days."

"Oh, okay," Jason said while bobbing his head.

"Can you make dinner for us tomorrow… Mr. Man?" Catalina asked politely while batting her eyelashes.

"Of course," Jason replied. "How about burgers and fries?"

"You're so classic, Jason. Bad to the bone!"

She gave him a kiss on the cheek and exited the vehicle. Jason smiled.

Chapter 12

Jason woke on the twelfth day to a pack of coyotes yelping outside his bedroom window. The sound came from the west, beyond his property. He lay in bed for a few extra minutes to enjoy the calls of nature. Then he rose and headed to the kitchen. He scooped some grounds for his morning cup.

Jason was excited to read from the Bible this morning. He walked with a bounce in his step out to the deck and down the stairs. To the stone podium that stood in the clearing of the pine grove.

Jason opened to Lamentations and read from chapter 3, verses 25–27:

The Lord is good to those who wait for him, to the soul who seeks him. It is good that one should wait quietly for the salvation of the Lord. It is good for a man that he bear the yoke in his youth.

On a material level, Jason had everything he needed and more. His novels became best sellers and brought him much wealth. He dabbled in screenwriting, and even music. He purchased Morning Glory *and* his new muscle car with cash. Money was no object for Jason.

But he did feel a yoke all along. He felt the yoke of loneliness.

He had *things.* He had a great career. So why the yoke?

Jason's loneliness manifested itself in the form of a three-day bender nearly three years ago in the City of Angels. Writer's block had hit him hard, and he decided to take his mind off his struggles by holing himself up in his bedroom with a year's supply of alcohol.

Jason unearthed some strange demons while on that bender, which concluded with him being thrown in jail and charged with a DUI. His blood-alcohol content on the third day of heavy drinking was off the charts, needless to say. Jason had gotten lucky his entire life as far as drinking and driving was concerned. But nearly three years ago, in the City of Angels, his luck ran dry.

Jason was now more than ready to remove the yoke. He yearned for a relationship with God, as well as an earthly relationship. Someone he could share the rest of his life with.

When Jason returned to the kitchen, he picked his phone up from the counter and noticed that he had a new text message from David.

Give me a call when you have a sec. Let's discuss that manuscript.

Jason took a big gulp. It was the moment of truth. What did David think of his testimony? He took a deep breath and made the call.

"Jason," David said in a sober tone, "how's it going, man?"

"Going great, David," Jason replied. "So… what did you think?"

There was silence on the other line. Then Jason heard David inhale and clear his throat.

"Well, buddy, I gotta say… that was some weird, wild stuff. I mean, the glowing cross, the angel, the bottomless pit. You saw *Jesus,* dude?"

"Yeah, I know it sounds unbelievable, but it all happened. And not just to me! My new friend Catalina has seen these things, too!" Jason asserted.

"Hmm, yeeeah, I don't know, Jason," David began. "It all seems a bit far-fetched. I know! Why don't you make it fiction! Create a character, Justin or Jacob or somebody, and say all these wild things happened to *him!* Then no one will think you're crazy. Okay?"

"That would be a total cop-out," Jason began, "and you know it. Look, you're missing the point here. These things are happening to me for a reason. As a writer, I have the ability and the platform to share my experiences with the world. The book is my testimony." There was silence on the other line for a few seconds. Then David spoke:

"To tell you the truth, I don't know if I could take this to All Terrene," David replied. "I mean, I'd be putting *my* neck on the line. Then I'd be the kook's agent. How would that make *me* look?"

Jason raised his eyebrows and paced through the room. Then he got an idea.

"Send it to a Christian publisher then," Jason proposed.

"No, no, no, dude," David responded quickly. "I only deal in the secular realm. The secular sphere, if you like. Much safer waters." Jason rolled his eyes.

"Can you just *try* and pitch it to All Terrene?" Jason pleaded. "They've published every book I've written so far."

Again, only silence could be heard on the other line. A few seconds passed.

"Okay, Jason," David agreed. "As a personal favor to you. Because you were my cash cow for all those years."

"Thank you, David," Jason responded dryly.

"Listen, I gotta go," David said. "I'll let you know what they say. Take it easy, dude."

With that, Jason tossed his phone on the sofa cushion. *Time to get some groceries,* he thought. *Dinner for three tonight.*

Catalina pulled into Jason's driveway just before eight o'clock. She put the Jeep in park and both her and her friend, Alma, walked up the stairs and to the kitchen door. Jason waved from inside the house and let them in.

"Jason Morrison!" Alma screamed. "The famous writer guy!"

Alma threw her arms around Jason. She was dressed in black and wearing perfume.

Jason also noticed she had a bottle of wine in her hand.

"Hi!" he said while gently hugging her back.

Catalina walked in and rolled her eyes.

"I brought some wine," Alma said. "Ooo, smells like cheeseburgers! And fries!"

Jason smiled and laid out a burger bar, complete with all the toppings, as well as a basket of homemade French fries.

"Help yourselves, ladies," Jason said.

The three of them sat at the dining room table and began to discuss the miraculous happenings. Alma looked over at Jason with a seductive smile.

"So, Jason," Alma began, "have you *really* seen all those crazy things? The glowing cross? The angel? The bottomless pit? *Jesus?*"

"Yes," Jason replied calmly. "I know it's hard to believe, but everything we've seen has actually happened. For real."

Jason glanced over at Catalina, who looked down and smiled.

"Oh, come *on!*" Alma shouted. "You put Catalina up to this. *Look!* She's smiling!"

Alma pointed her finger at Catalina. "I see her *smiling!*" The three of them began laughing together.

"She's just had too much *vino,*" Jason said with a deadpan delivery.

"Vino!" Alma screamed. "Did you just say *vino?*" They all started to laugh hysterically.

The burgers and fries went over great. Jason washed his back with several pints of beer.

Alma began to hike up her black dress as she danced around the living room. She was tan, like Catalina, and very attractive. Jason figured Catalina would have attractive friends.

"Let's go to the saloon!" Alma shouted. "The *salooon!"*

"Oh, no," Catalina snapped. "You're wasted."

Alma continued dancing and looked about the room. She looked toward the counter and her eyes grew wide. Just then, Alma made a dash for the counter and snatched the keys to the Jeep! She continued through the kitchen door and down the steps on the side of the house, stumbling on the way down.

"No!" Catalina cried as she raced after Alma.

Alma jumped inside the Jeep and started it quickly.

"No!" Catalina cried again as she hurried down the steps.

But she was too late. Alma put the Jeep in drive and sped off down the driveway. Jason looked on from the deck with a blank expression. The Jeep pulled onto the dirt road and took off toward the highway. Catalina slowed to a halt, looking on in utter disbelief. She turned around and yelled to Jason, who was still standing on the deck.

"Let's go!" she commanded. "We have to follow her! She's going to kill herself!"

"I can't drive," Jason stated from above. "I've had too much to drink."

"What?" Catalina shouted. "Are you kidding? You're fine!" Catalina peered into the garage. *"Let's go!"*

"I can't," Jason responded flatly. "I... I have a DUI on my record. I got it in L.A. three years ago."

Silence filled the air. Catalina paced around.

"Then I'll drive. Throw me your keys!" she instructed from the driveway below.

"No way, Catalina," Jason said. "It's not your car *and* you've been drinking."

"Ugh!" Catalina screamed while stomping her feet. She removed her phone from her pocket and began typing. "I can't believe you're making me do this!" she cried.

"What are you doing, Catalina?" Jason asked while looking down at her, still pacing in the driveway.

"I'm texting someone. I'm asking them for a ride!" she snapped.

Jason shook his head.

"Do you want me to come with you?"

"*No!*" Catalina shouted.

Jason threw his hands into the air and walked back inside the house.

About a half hour later, Jason could see a car pull into Catalina's driveway. Catalina ran to the passenger door and quickly got in. The vehicle took off down the dirt road and then turned onto the highway.

Jason shook his head.

Chapter 13

The thirteenth day at Morning Glory began with Jason being awoken by a strong breeze coming from his bedroom window. The night air was temperate. He moved his eyes around the room as a coyote called from the distance. A long primal howl that was carried by the wind.

Jason threw off his comforter and walked slowly to the kitchen.

Jason noticed that he was eager to read from the Bible each morning. He had so much to learn, or relearn. *This is what it feels like,* he thought, *to be living with Christ.* Each day was a new adventure for Jason.

He stepped out onto the deck and looked to Catalina's house. Her yellow Jeep was parked in the driveway, still intact. This gave Jason some relief. He walked down the steps and headed to the pine grove.

As Jason stepped into the clearing, he tilted his head back and observed the multitude of stars. Jason was regaining his sense of wonder out here in the wilderness. The stillness and majesty of his wild country plot was the perfect setting for his return to faith.

Jason turned to the Gospel according to Luke, and read from chapter 8, verses 43–48:

And there was a woman who had had a discharge of blood for twelve years, and though she had spent all her living on physicians, she could not be healed by anyone. She came up behind him and touched the fringe of his garment, and immediately her discharge of blood ceased. And Jesus said, "Who was it that touched me?" When all denied it, Peter said, "Master, the crowds surround you and are pressing in on you!" But Jesus said, "Someone touched me, for I perceive that power has gone out from me." And when the woman saw that she was not hidden, she came trembling, and falling down before him declared in the presence of all the people why she had touched him, and how she had been immediately healed. And he said to her, "Daughter, your faith has made you well; go in peace."

"If I could just touch the fringe of Christ's garment," Jason spoke aloud, "I would be immediately healed."

Jason yearned to rid himself of both his loneliness and anger. To go in peace wherever he went. The way he saw it, loneliness gave rise to anger. He desired a peaceful life so he could get things done. He wished to serve God while taking another soul along for the ride. Jason had been lonely for far too long. He knew he would need someone strong. Jason smiled. *I think I've found her,* he thought.

The sun was about to rise and Jason made his way back to the house. As he neared the driveway, he looked up and saw Catalina standing on the second-story deck above. She didn't look angry, which gave Jason some relief.

"Hey," she said sheepishly. "Can I talk to you?"

"Sure," he replied. "I'll meet you inside."

Jason and Catalina sat across from one another at the dining room table. Catalina took a deep breath and looked up at Jason.

"Sorry about last night," she began, "Alma is a wild child. I still can't believe she did that."

"No worries," Jason said. "I'm glad you're safe. And I'm glad the Jeep is in one piece."

Catalina chuckled.

"Yeah, no kidding." Catalina paused for a moment. "So, that was my friend Sam who came and picked me up after Alma kidnapped the Jeep."

"Sam?" Jason asked nervously.

"Yeah, her name is Samantha, we call her Sam," Catalina said.

Jason let out an internal sigh of relief. He tried his best to keep a poker face while Catalina continued.

"She lives in town. I told her what happened and she came right away. Her boyfriend was upset, though. This isn't the first time that Sam and I have had to babysit Alma and clean up her mess."

"I see," Jason said.

"When Sam and I got to the saloon, Alma was even drunker and hitting on some biker. The gang was buying her shots and laughing behind her back. You should have seen the way they were looking at her. It was creepy."

Jason raised his eyebrows. Catalina continued:

"Sam and I had to drag her out of there, which pissed off the bikers. They saw an easy target. Who knows what would have happened if Sam and I weren't there?"

"You're a good friend," Jason started, "but it sounds like trouble follows Alma. Or Alma seeks trouble, one of the two."

"Yeah," Catalina replied, "she likes to have fun. You're right, though. Her impulsive nature ruins it for others. As Sam and I were dragging her out of the saloon, one of those dirty bikers slapped me on the butt."

Jason furrowed his brow.

"Which one?" he asked.

Catalina could sense a sudden change in Jason's demeanor. She could see that same crazed look come over his face. She noticed that he was now breathing heavier and faster.

"Um," she began hesitantly, "the one with the gold tooth. I could see it flash in the light as he was sneering at me with that devilish look."

"The one with the gold tooth," Jason whispered. "Hmm."

Catalina could feel his anger. It was palpable. She decided to change the subject.

"I shouldn't have asked you to drive. I'm sorry. You could have been pulled over by a cop and who knows what would have happened..."

"Unfortunately, I know all too well what would have happened," Jason said shamefully.

"I would have been thrown in jail."

Catalina looked down. Jason continued:

"It's okay. I know it's awkward, but yes, I got a DUI when I lived in Los Angeles. I spent the night in a cell with six other men. It smelled like piss." Catalina let out a sigh.

"It was costly and embarrassing," Jason admitted. He let the words hang in the air for a moment. "But I'll tell you this: I have never driven a car drunk since!" Catalina raised her head and cracked a slight smile.

"Really?" she asked in a shaky voice.

"Really," Jason replied with pride. "It was a wake-up call. I mean, I still imbibe from time to time, I just don't get in a car and drive."

Jason felt a weight lift from his shoulders. It felt good to tell Catalina the truth. It felt good to share his pain with another person. And not just any person—his new best friend. Jason felt comfortable sharing his experience with Catalina. She soothed him.

"That's great, Jason," Catalina said. "I'm so happy for you!"

Catalina rose from her chair at the table and walked to Jason. She threw her arms around him and squeezed tightly. Jason put his arms around her back and the pair embraced.

"Anyway," Catalina said as she pulled away, wiping a tear from her cheek, "we got home safely. Alma did throw up in my front yard, though. All in the grass." Jason laughed heartily.

"Oh, Alma, whatever shall we do with you?" he joked.

The afternoon sun was high in the sky and Jason was once again sitting on his deck overlooking the meadow and tall grass below him. He was glad he told Catalina about his past. It was time to move forward. He looked eastward toward the mountain and held his gaze. Then he remembered something Catalina said earlier. How the biker with the gold tooth had slapped her on the butt at the old saloon last night.

Jason's chest heaved forward as he took a deep breath. He began to feel his heart beating faster. The left side of his mouth raised in a snarl. The anger was growing by the second.

Peace, dude, he recited internally, *keep your peace, dude.*

Jason rose quickly and walked to the railing. He put both his hands on the top rail and took another deep breath.

"It's not worth it," Jason said aloud.

He imagined the biker with the gold tooth touching Catalina and then sneering with that devilish look on his face. Jason tried his best to extinguish the anger, but it won out.

Jason descended the steps and made his way to the garage. He began rifling through cardboard boxes in search of something. The crazed look had returned to his eyes.

A few moments later, Jason pulled a small bat-like object from one of the boxes. It was his billy club. He gripped the hardwood in his right hand and tapped the club on his left palm.

He raised it high and admired the lacquered finish. Then he got in his Challenger.

Jason headed south down the highway at a furious pace. His billy club sat beside him on the passenger seat. He began to formulate a plan of action in his mind. He visualized walking in the saloon, seating himself on the left side of the bar, and staking out his prey.

"Hopefully Mr. Gold Tooth is in today," Jason said in a sinister tone.

As he pulled into the saloon's parking lot, he counted the bikes lined up near the entrance. Fifteen. *Do these guys ever do anything without each other?* he pondered.

Jason parked his Challenger near the back of the lot. There was only one other car there—a long white luxury car a few spaces ahead. Jason grabbed his billy club, squeezed it in his right hand, and exited the vehicle.

Jason sported a black leather jacket for the occasion, which allowed him to tuck the club inside the left breast pocket. He had to be inconspicuous. As he walked to the entrance, he took a deep breath while raising his shoulders up and down.

"Let's *go!*" he roared.

He entered the old saloon and its familiar stench hit him in the face. A ghastly combination of beer-soaked wooden floors, tobacco smoke, and urine. Very sulfuric.

Jason seated himself at the left side of the counter. He saw the old barkeeper amble out of the back room with his same hunched posture. When the old man noticed Jason, his eyes grew wide and he let out a grunt.

"Didn't think I'd ever see you back here again!" the old barkeeper barked while brushing strands of gray hair from his face. "What can I get you, *friend?*"

As the words left his mouth, the familiar devilish grin crept over his face.

"I'll have a Coke," Jason answered.

The barkeeper grunted and began to walk away.

"Hey," Jason began in a friendly manner, "is our friend with the gold tooth here today?"

The old man turned around and pointed to the opposite end of the counter. There sat Mr. Gold Tooth, yucking it up with his cronies. Jason looked in his direction with a stoic stare. He noticed his black vest was not adorned with a 666 patch. The man across the bar then noticed Jason and smiled. His gold tooth gleamed in the light. Jason unzipped his jacket and gently felt the billy club in his right hand.

An older gentleman in a black blazer approached the bar at that moment. He pulled out a stool to Jason's right.

"Mind if I sit here?" the gentleman asked politely.

"Not at all, sir," Jason replied.

A sense of calm then came over Jason. He didn't know why, but the gentleman's presence had shifted his mood. Jason was tranquil. His violent urge was temporarily subdued.

The barkeeper returned with Jason's Coke.

"Three dollars!" he shouted.

Jason threw down a five-dollar bill.

"Keep the change, *friend,*" Jason said.

The barkeeper snatched the bill and looked at the gentleman.

"What'll it be?" he asked.

"I'll have what he's having," the gentleman stated.

The barkeeper rolled his eyes and walked away. Jason grabbed the glass and took a drink of cola. He then zipped up his jacket in a quick move.

"You don't have to do that, Jason," the gentleman said in a steady tone.

Jason turned and looked at the man to his right. The gentleman had a short-cropped gray beard. The hair on top of his head was neatly combed and slicked back. He had a dignified air about him.

"How do you know my name, sir?" Jason asked.

"Oh, you're famous around these parts," the gentleman stated. "The famous fiction writer from Los Angeles. The one with the beautiful girlfriend." The gentleman winked his left eye at Jason.

"She *is* beautiful," Jason said.

"You don't want to lose your cool and throw it all away, dude. You've got a beautiful new girlfriend, a nice place, and a sweet ride. Plus, I hear you're writing a new book."

Jason's eyes began to well with tears. The barkeeper then returned with the gentleman's cola. The gentleman also dropped a five-dollar bill on the counter.

"Keep the change," he said.

The barkeeper snatched the bill and walked away slowly. He returned to the back room while looking over his shoulder at Jason and the gentleman.

"Are you an angry man, Jason?" the gentleman asked calmly.

Jason pondered the question for a moment. He wanted to give a thoughtful response.

"I can be," Jason started. "It gets the better of me sometimes. I hate to see good people get taken advantage of. And I hate bullies."

"Me too, dude," the gentleman said. "But if we had to take a billy club to every bully, we'd never get anything done."

Jason laughed and cracked a big smile.

"I forgot to ask, what's your name, sir?" Jason asked the gentleman.

"My name's Al," he replied, extending his right hand. Jason shook Al's hand and felt a gentle current of electricity run through his body.

"Nice to meet you, Al," Jason replied with a smile. "Thanks for cooling me down."

"Anytime, dude… anytime."

Just then, the backroom door swung open and out came an old man with a weather-beaten face. He was wearing a black vest adorned with a 666 patch. He was sporting Coke-bottle glasses and a flat top. It was the leader of the 666 gang himself: Bill Banner.

"Well, well!" the old man shouted across the room. "If it isn't the famous writer from Los Angle-eeze! Jason Morrison! We saw yer broad here last night. Scooter here even had himself a feel!"

Bill grabbed Scooter by the shoulders and laughed. Scooter flashed a smile, exposing his gold tooth. The rest of the gang laughed heartily in unison while sporting devilish grins. Jason did his best to remain calm.

"What's in yer jacket?" Bill shouted across the room. He was looking directly at Jason.

"You was reachin' in your jacket earlier. Old Johnny Boy here told me all about it!"

Bill then took his right hand and put it on the barkeeper's shoulder. Johnny Boy was the barkeep. Johnny Boy had tattled on Jason.

"What's in yer *jacket?*" Bill screamed.

Jason stood to his feet and unzipped his jacket. He pulled a lacquered billy club out in his right hand and raised it into the air.

"A *club?*" Bill shouted. "This guy brings a *club?*"

The gang flanking Bill began to laugh loudly. All the men were sporting devilish grins.

The laughing continued for several seconds.

"We got *guns* here!" Bill yelled, looking from left to right. "Ain't that right, boys?" Bill's gang raised their vests and displayed pistols at their waists.

At that moment, the gentleman, Al, flanked Jason on the right. He pulled a sawed-off, double-barrel shotgun from his black blazer and pointed it at the gang. Some took a step back, while others reached for their pistols.

"Ah, ah, ah," Al said while shaking his head. "Anyone draws and I'll blast all of you."

The gang stood motionless and looked to Bill for guidance. Bill stood frozen, speechless for the first time.

"Walk backward to the door, Jason," Al instructed. "I'll cover you."

Jason took several steps back and peered over his shoulder. The door was close. Al began backpedaling as well, shotgun still pointed at the gang.

"You boys ever come back, you're *dead!*" Bill shouted, adjusting his Coke-bottle glasses.

Jason kicked the door open with his heel and stepped outside. He held the door open and Al backed out slowly, gun still drawn.

"Alright, let's get out of here," Al said.

The two men hurried to the back of the lot with smiles on their faces. Al went to his long white luxury car and

Jason to his black Challenger. A few bikers came out of the saloon and stood by the entrance, incensed.

"Remember, dude, go in peace," Al instructed as he opened the door to his car.

"Bye, Al!" Jason said with a smile across his face.

The two men jumped into their respective vehicles and sped off. Jason turned onto the highway and began heading north, back to Morning Glory. He glanced in his rearview mirror and saw the white luxury car turn onto the highway and begin heading south.

Jason couldn't stop smiling as he drove away to safety.

Chapter 14

Jason woke to a cooing sound on the fourteenth morning. It wasn't coming from far away, but nearby. He looked to the window and saw two birds sitting on the window ledge.

Then, he heard the familiar cooing sound again. They were doves!

Jason sat up in bed slowly, so as not to frighten them. The doves pattered their small feet along the ledge, occasionally embracing one another. Jason watched silently from his bed.

Coo coo-coo! The sound of the doves filled his bedroom. For a few more moments, Jason sat there and watched the birds. Then, suddenly, they flew away in unison.

As Jason walked to the clearing in the pine grove, he felt a warm sensation come over him. It was peaceful and radiated throughout his entire body.

Once in the clearing, Jason looked up and saw the moon shining brightly. The stars were plentiful and the night sky a deep black.

"Thank you," Jason whispered.

He stooped down and opened the chest. Jason pulled the headlamp out first and adjusted it atop his head. Then he removed the Holy Bible and gently placed it on the stone's shelf.

Jason pressed the button on the headlamp and out poured the artificial light. Jason moved the ray of light over the Bible, and selected a passage from the Song of Solomon, chapter 2, verses 8–12:

The voice of my beloved! Behold, he comes, leaping over the mountains, bounding over the hills. My beloved is like a gazelle or a young stag. Behold, there he stands behind our wall, gazing through the windows, looking through the lattice. My beloved speaks and says to me: "Arise, my love, my beautiful one, and come away, for behold, the winter is past; the rain is over and gone. The flowers appear on the earth, the time of singing has come, and the voice of the turtledove is heard in our land."

A melody began to play in Jason's head. He hummed it to himself and then found the words.

"Catalina, senorita, you were sent from above," Jason began to sing aloud. "Catalina, senorita, our language is love."

It was a nice melody with lots of potential. Jason continued to hum as he strolled back to Morning Glory.

As Jason walked through the living area, he picked up his phone from the end table. He had a new text message from Catalina:

Hey! I'm driving Alma back to the airport. Hope you get some good writing done today!

Jason replied:

Hey Catalina! Safe travels. Can you join me for dinner tonight? I'm making my signature dish: scallops marinara.

A few seconds passed. *Ding!*

Sure! How about seven o'clock?

Jason replied:

Seven is great! See you then!

Catalina replied with a smiling emoji.

As the morning sun ascended into the sky, a great idea came to Jason. He went down to the guest bedroom on the first floor and walked to the corner. Jason lifted his acoustic guitar from its stand. He gave it a strum and winced.

"Needs to be tuned," he whispered.

Jason tuned the beautiful instrument and gave it another strum. A C major chord.

"There we go," he said happily.

Aside from being a novelist, Jason was also an accomplished songwriter. In fact, he had penned many hits for many different musicians.

His first hit song was 'Can't Force a Feeling', a slow rock number with a forceful backbeat. Jason penned the song—complete with lyrics, melody, and chords—and gave it to one of his closest friends in Los Angeles. A budding young musician with flowing red hair named Bethany. Sure enough, it worked. The song rose up the charts and catapulted Bethany's career.

Jason officially became a hit songwriter!

More hits would follow over the years. There was his foray into psychedelic pop, 'She Plays with My Head'. The dark, candle-lit anthem, 'Six Feet Under'. There was the bright and hopeful classic, 'See It in Your Eyes'. And, of course, the irresistibly seductive serenade known as 'Nights and White Chocolate'.

Jason never joined a band; he preferred to write the songs behind-the-scenes. People were often shocked when they found out Jason had penned some of their favorite tunes. *"Really?"* they would ask quizzically. "Jason Morrison, the author dude, wrote those songs?"

Yep. Jason Morrison was also an accomplished songwriter.

Jason then set the acoustic guitar back on the stand. He moved to the other corner of the guest bedroom and approached the dresser. He opened the top drawer. There it was: his stash of herb.

Jason rolled a joint, grabbed his guitar, and headed back to the pine grove. This morning he felt inspired.

Jason walked to the center of the clearing and leaned his guitar against the stone podium.

He lit his joint and sat down in the grass. Between puffs, Jason began to hum the new melody. He recalled the words and began to sing them aloud:

"Catalina, senorita, you were sent from above. Catalina, senorita, our language is love." He paused, then added another line:

"You don't need to, but if you want to, you can speak my tongue. Catalina, senorita, our language is love."

Jason smiled contentedly and took another drag from his joint. He blew the white smoke into the air above. He had entered a state of meditation. Jason observed each moment consciously.

He continued to ride the wave of inspiration and stood up to fetch his acoustic guitar. Jason then leaned his back against the stone podium and cradled the guitar in his arms. He propped the body of the instrument up with his left leg. His left hand fretted a C major chord and his right hand strummed the strings. It was in tune. Jason then strummed an F major chord.

And then a G major chord.

C   F   G

Catalina, senorita, you were sent from above

C   F   G

Catalina, senorita, our language is love

C   F   G

You don't need to, but if you want to, you can speak my tongue

C   F   G

Catalina, senorita, our language is love

F   G   C

And all that I can do is play your game

F   G   C

Run around just like a clown all day

F   G

That's what you do to me, whoa oh

                            C

Catalina

Jason inadvertently added a verse to go along with the chorus.

"Cool," he whispered.

Jason continued to play his guitar in the pine grove until a sleepiness came over him. A nap seemed like the perfect idea. He walked back to Morning Glory with guitar in hand and headed off to the master bedroom.

As Jason lifted his eyelids and emerged from his nap, he could hear the familiar cooing again. The pair of doves had returned to his windowsill and were singing. Their tiny feet pattering across the ledge. He watched them embrace, rolling their necks around each other and purring. A few moments later, they were gone. Jason headed to the shower.

Once dressed, he headed to the supermarket. Tonight's meal would be very special. His signature dish: scallops marinara.

As his black Challenger cruised down the highway, he went over the list of ingredients in his head. *Scallops, angel hair pasta, marinara sauce, spinach, and bacon.* His mouth began to salivate. *And some wine. For good measure.*

When he arrived at Shopper's Club, he kept his eyes peeled for any gang members. No motorcycles in the parking lot. No devilish men.

He strolled down the aisles of the supermarket humming his newly-created tune.

"Catchy," he admitted.

Jason checked out and happily strolled back to his muscle car. No motorcycles. No gang members revving their engines.

At seven o'clock sharp, Catalina walked up the steps on the side of Morning Glory.

Jason saw her approach the kitchen door and waved.

Catalina walked in and Jason was immediately spellbound. She was wearing a blue dress with white high-heel shoes. Her lips were full and red; her eyes a deep brown. Her long black hair fell down her back in waves. And her skin was tan, radiant.

"Wow!" Jason exclaimed aloud.

Catalina laughed and blushed slightly.

"Smells good in here," she said as she raised her nose in the air.

"It's almost ready. Have a seat," Jason implored.

As Catalina walked to the dining room table, she noticed the acoustic guitar leaning against the sofa.

"You play guitar?" she asked.

"Yep," Jason replied. "I wrote you a song."

"Really?" Catalina said with a puzzled look.

"Yep," Jason replied confidently. "I'll play it for you after dinner."

Catalina smiled and sat down at the table. Jason served two plates of scallops marinara (with bacon sprinkled on top) and poured two glasses of wine. The pair toasted to good times and new adventures.

"Mmm, this is so good!" Catalina said. "Author and chef!"

"And musician," Jason added. "I've written some hits you probably didn't even know were mine."

"Really?" Catalina said bewilderedly. "Like what?"

"Ever heard the song 'Can't Force a Feeling'?" Jason asked. *"Yes!"* Catalina squealed. "By Bethany Gatore! I love that song!"

"I wrote that. The words and music," Jason said with pride.

"No way!" Catalina responded skeptically.

"Look it up," he urged. "Check the songwriting credit."

Catalina grabbed her phone in a quick move and began to type furiously. A few moments later, a look of sheer surprise came over her face. Her mouth dropped.

"Oh my God!" she said with a smile. "Words and music by Jason Morrison. That's *you!"*

Jason laughed out loud.

"Ever heard the song 'Six Feet Under'?" Jason asked.

"Yes!" Catalina cried. "You wrote 'Six Feet Under'? The one by Peter Tettleton?"

"Yep," Jason said with a confident smile.

Catalina typed away furiously on her phone.

"No *way!* Words and music by *Jason Morrison!"* Catalina said in utter disbelief.

"Author, chef, *and* songwriter. You're a magic man, Jason! A magic man!"

"Well," Jason began, "I don't know about *magic man…* but I am pretty good."

"Play my song!" Catalina squealed.

A giant smile crossed Jason's face. He took a gulp of wine and then headed over to his acoustic guitar. He sat on the sofa and strummed a C major chord. Catalina walked over and sat down on the other sofa while sipping from her wine glass. Jason then strummed an F major chord. And then a G major chord. Catalina smiled while peeking over her glass. Jason took a deep breath and began playing:

C   F   G

Catalina, senorita, you were sent from above

C   F   G

Catalina, senorita, our language is love

C   F   G

You don't need to, but if you want to, you can speak my tongue

        C   F   G

Catalina, senorita, our language is love

  F   G   C

And all that I can do is sit and wait

  F   G   C

Feet on the ground, won't move around all day

  F   G

That's what you do to me, whoa oh

                              C

Catalina

As Jason strummed the final chord, the room fell silent. He noticed he had inadvertently added a second verse. He smiled on the inside. Catalina sat across from him on the other sofa, wide-eyed.

"Wow," she said calmly. "You *are* good."

"Thanks," Jason replied graciously. "That will be a hit someday." Catalina smiled and blushed.

As the night drew to a close, Jason and Catalina found themselves in the kitchen. They were chatting and looking at each other while trying to hold back laughter.

When the moment was right, Jason moved in and placed his hands on Catalina's hips. He then pressed his lips to hers and the two began kissing passionately. Jason noticed how great Catalina smelled and pulled on her lower lip. She moaned and breathed in through her nose.

Just then, Jason pulled away and looked into Catalina's eyes.

"Catalina… will you be my girlfriend?" Jason asked in a confident tone.

"Yes," she replied happily.

Chapter 15

Jason woke to the sound of silence on the morning of the fifteenth day at Morning Glory. He gazed up at the ceiling fan and smiled. A gentle breeze blew through the open bedroom window. It was cool and refreshing. Jason could smell a hint of pine. He threw the comforter to the side and walked slowly to the kitchen.

"Good morning," Jason announced.

At that moment, Catalina spun around in place, slightly startled. She caught her breath and smiled. Jason noticed two ceramic mugs sitting next to one another on the counter.

"I'm making coffee," Catalina said. "Want some?"

"Absolutely," Jason replied.

Jason and Catalina took their mugs to the deck and sat side-by-side, facing the great mountain. They sat and talked until the sun rose over the right shoulder of the mountain. The pair took in the beautiful view before them to the east. The grassy meadow. The hill. And the great mountain. Humphreys Peak.

"Want to read a Bible passage?" Jason asked Catalina.

"Sure," she agreed. "You can read it, though. I like your deep voice."

The duo headed to the pine grove and stopped in the middle of the clearing. Jason opened the wooden chest and lifted the Bible out. He placed it on the stone podium and read a passage from the Letter to the Hebrews. Chapter 10, verses 19–25:

Therefore, brothers, since we have confidence to enter the holy places by the blood of Jesus, by the new and living way that he opened for us through the curtain, that is, through his flesh, and since we have a great priest over the house of God, let us draw near with a true heart in full assurance of faith, with our hearts sprinkled clean from an evil conscience and our bodies washed with pure water. Let us hold fast the confession of our hope without wavering, for he who promised is faithful. And let us consider how to stir up one another to love and good works, not neglecting to meet together, as is the habit of some, but encouraging one another, and all the more as you see the day drawing near.

"We're stirring up good works, Catalina," Jason said as he looked at her. "Our testimony will come at a cost, though. Not everyone is agreeable to the way of Jesus Christ."

"We need believers in our lives," she responded with assurance. "People of faith. That is who our testimony is for."

Just then, Catalina reached into her pocket and pulled her phone out. She glanced down and smiled.

"Oh good, they're coming over tonight," Catalina said while looking down at her phone.

"Who's coming over tonight?" Jason asked.

Catalina looked up while still sporting a smile.

"Grandma," she began, "and my parents. Oh, and my younger brother, Hernan." Jason's eyes grew wide. He was going to meet the parents. Mr. and Mrs.…

"Hey," Jason started, "what's your last name?" Catalina chuckled.

"Cabrera," she responded.

"Cabrera," Jason repeated. "Catalina Cabrera. Wow. What a great name. What are your parents' names?" he asked.

"Sergio and Sofia," she replied. "You should probably call them Mr. and Mrs. Cabrera, though."

"Of course," Jason said.

"Can you make dinner? Around seven?" Catalina asked politely.

"Sure," he replied. "How about pizza?"

"Sounds great," she said. "You can be the chef tonight, Mr. Famous Author… slash Songwriter."

At seven o'clock, Jason spotted Catalina and her family walking up his driveway. They began up the stairs on the side of the house, single file. Jason opened the kitchen door and held it open for the Cabrera's.

Grandma Maria came through the door first and gave Jason a big smile. Next, Catalina walked in wearing a short black dress. Following her came Sergio and Sofia. Mr. and Mrs. Cabrera. Mr. Cabrera was sporting a dark blue polo shirt and Bermuda shorts. He had black hair and was several inches shorter than Jason. *Small, dark, and handsome,* Jason quipped to himself. Mrs. Cabrera walked in next wearing a short red dress. Very Jessica Rabbit. She was about the same height as Catalina, but she possessed a bit more curvature. The last to walk in the door was Hernan, Catalina's brother. He looked about the same age as Catalina. Hernan stood tall with a mane of curly brown hair.

"Welcome, everyone!" Jason began. "Help yourselves to pizza and beer." Jason leaned in and spoke into the back of his right hand while twiddling his fingers, "And a little *vino* for the ladies..." This line made Jason chuckle to himself.

The room fell silent. The Cabrera's all squinted their eyes at Jason. You could hear a pin drop.

"Very interesting, Jason," Mr. Cabrera remarked. *"Very* interesting."

Jason and the Cabrera's sat around the dining room table. Jason made two large pizzas; one with pepperoni and black olives, and the other with sausage and onion. It was a hit. The men drank beer and the women enjoyed their wine. Laughter and good conversation were plentiful that evening.

"So, Jason," Mr. Cabrera began, "what was it like seeing Jesus crucified on the cross?" Jason took a swig of beer from his glass and thought the question over.

"Amazing," Jason answered. "My heart ached the first time I saw him crucified. The second time, when I went with Catalina, I stared in awe. It was at night. His body was illuminated by a small fire that burned wild on the banks of the lake."

Mr. Cabrera looked over at Catalina. She smiled at her dad and nodded her head.

"Wow!" Hernan exclaimed. "You're so lucky, Jason!"

"Tell them about your other vision, Jason," Grandma Maria implored. "The one you and Catalina had at the park… you know, the pit."

"Oh, yeah!" Jason remembered. "Catalina and I went to the park one morning and saw a pit appear before our very eyes. Grass and dirt swirled around and then collapsed into a deep hole. A pit. A bottomless pit!"

Sofia gasped.

"Cool!" Hernan shouted.

"I also saw an angel appear in that very same spot at the park," Jason stated. "It was breathtaking. She was surrounded by a brilliant white aura."

Grandma Maria smiled and took a sip from her wine glass.

"I *loved* your novel, *Desperate Times in the West,* Jason," Sofia said in an alluring tone.

She shot Jason a look as she took a sip from her glass.

Jason raised his eyebrows. He looked around the table and saw Catalina glaring at him.

He took a swig of beer.

After dinner, Jason decided to play some music and keep the party going. He had a sound system built into the walls. *What a perfect opportunity to try it out.*

Jason selected the seductive rock hit known as 'Nights and White Chocolate', by Joseph Perry Jackson. As the song began playing, Sofia strutted to the center of the living area and started dancing.

"Woo!" Sofia exclaimed. "I *love* this song!"

Jason looked over at Catalina. He could read her lips as she silently mouthed the words, *You wrote this?*

Jason nodded and silently mouthed the word, *Yep.*

"Woo! Woo woo!" Sofia exclaimed as she moved her hips from left to right. "Look, Sergio! I'm a train. *Woo woo!"*

Sergio looked at Jason and smiled.

"She's a handful, Jason," Sergio said in an even voice. "A real handful." Jason took a sip of beer from his glass.

"Come *dance* with me, Jason Morrison!" Sofia shouted from across the room. "Come *dance* with me, Mr. Famous Author!"

Jason raised his eyebrows and pouted his lips. He noticed Sergio out of the corner of his eye. He was staring at Jason.

"Do you want to dance with my wife, Jason?" Sergio asked sternly.

Jason's eyes grew wide. He thought the question over.

"Um… no," he replied hesitantly.

The air was filled with silence.

"Why not?" Sergio asked, still staring at Jason.

"Woo woo!" Sofia shouted as she danced through the room. "Come *dance* with me, Jason Morrison!"

Jason couldn't take his eyes off Sofia, who was moving her hips from left to right in a short red dress with a glass of wine in her hand. Then, he looked back at Sergio.

"Um… I like your daughter, Sergio. I mean… Mr. Cabrera," Jason replied.

Sergio continued to stare at Jason. The silence was deafening.

"Hey Jason!" Hernan called, standing by the kitchen door. "Show me the stone podium!" Jason looked back at Sergio, who was still staring at him.

"Excuse me, Mr. Cabrera," Jason said.

Hernan opened the door and the two walked out to the deck.

"You have a great house, Jason," Hernan said.

"Thank you," Jason replied graciously.

The two walked down the stairs. Jason led the way to the pine grove. As they came upon the clearing, Hernan spotted the giant stone rising from the earth.

"Whoa!" he cried. Hernan ran toward the stone and noticed the wooden chest lying on the ground next to the stone. He looked back at Jason.

"What's in the chest?" Hernan asked.

"My Bible," Jason answered, "and a headlamp. I come out here and read Bible passages before dawn. With a headlamp on."

"Cool!" Hernan replied enthusiastically.

"I lay the Bible right here," Jason said, as he pointed to the shelf at the top of the stone.

"Can I read a passage, Jason?" Hernan asked.

"Be my guest," Jason replied.

Hernan opened the chest and lifted the Bible from inside. He began flipping through the book furiously. Jason sensed that he knew the contents well. He stopped at the Gospel according to Matthew and set the Bible on the natural shelf. Hernan read aloud from chapter 23, verses 1–12:

Then Jesus said to the crowds and to his disciples, "The scribes and the Pharisees sit on Moses' seat, so do and observe whatever they tell you, but not the works they do. For they preach, but do not practice. They tie up heavy burdens, hard to bear, and lay them on people's shoulders, but they themselves are not willing to move them with their finger. They do all their deeds to be seen by others. For they make their phylacteries broad and their fringes long, and they love the place of honor at feasts and the best seats in the synagogues and greetings in the marketplaces and being called rabbi by others. But you are not to be called rabbi, for you have one teacher, and you are all brothers. And call no man your father on earth, for you have one Father, who is in heaven. Neither be called instructors, for you have one instructor, the Christ. The greatest among you shall be your servant. Whoever exalts himself will be humbled, and whoever humbles himself will be exalted.

"That was great, Hernan," Jason said. "Thank you."

"You're welcome," Hernan replied. He closed the book and returned it to the chest. "So how old are you, dude?"

Jason was taken aback at the sudden shift in topic.

"Uh, thirty-six," Jason answered. "Thirty-six years *young.* I like to say that I'm in my… fertile stomping grounds."

Jason amused himself with the line and chuckled. Hernan stood unfazed.

"How old are you, Hernan?" he asked.

"Twenty-one," Hernan answered. "Two years younger than my sister… Catalina… who is twenty-three. Don't you think that's a bit odd, dude?"

Jason stood perplexed. He didn't expect to be put on the spot.

"Uh… what's odd, Hernan?" Jason asked.

"That you're thirty-six years old and dating my sister… who's twenty-three years *young?"*

Hernan's comment was a hit, but it did not sink Jason's battleship.

"Well," Jason began, "your grandmother, Maria, says that I'm young at heart, so… *rarr!"*

Jason made a pawing motion with both hands like a tiger. Silence filled the air.

Hernan's facial expression did not change. He simply stared at Jason with a deadpan gaze.

"Very interesting, dude," Hernan said. *"Very* interesting."

A few minutes later, Jason and Hernan rejoined the party. As they walked into the kitchen, Sofia spotted Jason and ran in his direction.

"Jason!" Sofia shouted. "You never told me that you were a *songwriter* as well! My daughter just told me about all your hits. You're a magic man, Jason Morrison! A magic man!" Jason chuckled and blushed.

"We better be getting home, Catalina," Mr. Cabrera said. "Nice to meet you, Jason."

Mr. Cabrera extended his right hand in Jason's direction.

"Nice to meet you, Mr. Cabrera," Jason replied while shaking his hand.

Maria then approached Jason, beaming a great smile.

"May God be with you," Grandma Maria said as she hugged Jason. He held her tight and smiled.

Sofia then walked toward Jason seductively in her red dress.

"Goodnight, Jason," Sofia said. She threw her arms around him and he held her tight.

"Goodnight, Sofia," Jason said.

Hernan then approached Jason with a smile on his face.

"Bye, Jason!" Hernan said. "It was nice meeting you." Hernan extended his right hand.

"Nice meeting you, Hernan," Jason said as he shook his hand.

Finally, Catalina walked up to Jason. She strutted toward him in her short black dress. Her hair was in a ponytail and she stared at him with her deep brown eyes. She was wearing red high-heel shoes. *Oh, senorita!* he thought.

"Goodnight, Jason," Catalina said as she kissed him on the cheek. "Thanks for another *wonderful* evening."

Jason smiled and leaned into her ear.

"You look *amazing,*" he whispered.

Catalina grinned and walked to the kitchen door. She glanced at Jason as she headed out to the deck.

Chapter 16

The sixteenth day at Morning Glory began with Jason waking from a dream.

In his dream, Jason stood on the banks of the lake beyond the hill. He stared out across the water and stood motionless. A few birds sailed over the water.

Just then, Jason heard someone approaching from over his right shoulder.

"How's it going, dude?" a deep voice asked.

Jason turned and saw a man come up slowly from behind him. It was the gentleman. It was Al.

"Al!" Jason shouted. "How are you?"

Al smiled and looked down at the mud and stone mixture at the edge of the lake. His feet sank into the ground.

"I'm good, Jason." Al replied. "How are *you* doing?"

"I'm *great!*" Jason responded enthusiastically.

Jason's joy made Al crack another smile.

"I heard Catalina is officially your girlfriend now," Al began. "Way to go, dude. Way to go."

Tears welled up in Jason's eyes as the words left Al's mouth.

"Yeah," Jason replied. "She's beautiful."

Al nodded his head and then looked out over the open water. He fixed his gaze upon the great mountain.

"I know you've been lonely, Jason," Al stated. "You deserve this."

Jason stared straight ahead. He looked to the mountain in awe. Al continued:

"God loves you, Jason. He believes in you. He needs you to continue to spread the word of his Son, Jesus Christ. He needs you to take on that mantle. Can you do that for him?"

"Absolutely," Jason responded without hesitation.

"I'm glad to hear you say that," Al said. "Your testimony will strengthen people's faith. The world needs a man like you."

Jason was flattered by Al's kind words.

"I hope I can live up to his expectations," Jason said.

Al and Jason stared out over the water. It was serene. Placid.

"I have to go now, Jason," Al stated. "Be good to Catalina."

Just then, Jason woke from his dream. This time, it was a very pleasant dream. He lay in his bed for a few minutes, taking in what he had just experienced. It was moving. The gentleman had tugged at his soul.

Jason sprung out of bed and made his way to the kitchen. The hardwood was cool beneath his feet. He started the coffee maker and headed straight to the pine grove. To the stone podium at the center of the clearing.

He decided to read a passage from the First Letter of Peter. Chapter 4, verses 12–16:

Beloved, do not be surprised at the fiery trial when it comes upon you to test you, as though something strange were happening to you. But rejoice insofar as you share Christ's sufferings, that you may also rejoice and be glad when his glory is revealed. If you are insulted for the name of Christ, you are blessed, because the Spirit of glory and of God rests upon you. But let none of you suffer as a murderer or a thief or an evildoer or as a meddler. Yet if anyone suffers as a Christian, let him not be ashamed, but let him glorify God in that name.

Jason was prepared for his fiery trial. He knew that his Christian faith would exclude him from certain circles. But the things Jason had seen while at Morning Glory were far too powerful to be kept a secret.

"Even if some abandon me," Jason said aloud, "I know that God will put faithful people in their place."

But why me? Jason thought. *Why did God choose me for this mission?*

The first thing that came to mind was his embrace of the Spirit. He always felt something there. He conversed with the Spirit. Even though he didn't fully realize it, Jason had had a personal relationship with God all along.

Second, his life was his testimony. A man raised in the church who wandered. A lost sheep. His arrival at Morning Glory was no coincidence. It was the shepherd calling his lost sheep back to the flock.

Third, he had a platform. As an established author, Jason could spread his testimony through the written word.

The last thing he thought of was his righteous nature. Not perfect nature, but righteous nature. Jason always strived to default on righteousness. He didn't bully or instigate. He didn't cut others down, but instead supported them. Jason always maintained a positive outlook, even when he was around shady people. He felt being evil was taking the easy way out; for good people are often mocked. The way of righteousness is more difficult than it appears. One is met with resistance at every turn.

Then Jason thought about his past misdeeds. Could he really take up this mantle with so many past misdeeds? He swore, he fornicated, he hurt people, and he didn't even go to church regularly. But maybe that would change? Maybe that's what really brought him to Morning Glory?

Jason left the pine grove and walked back to his house. He fetched his cup of jo and glanced at his phone on the end table. Jason felt a dark foreboding. He walked to his phone and picked it up. He had a new text message from David.

Hey Jason. Call me this morning. Gotta talk business.

Jason took a deep breath. He knew this moment was inevitable. Before thinking about it too much, he called David.

"Jason," David said in a flat tone, "how are you doing today, man?"

"I'm doing well, David," he replied.

"Good, good… well, I gave the manuscript to All Terrene, as a favor to you, and they didn't know what to make of it, buddy. At first, they thought it was a joke. Then I told them that you're serious." David paused. "Then they looked at me like *I* was nuts, dude! You really put me in a bind, my man."

"Well, I didn't mean to put you in a bind," Jason said. "All of those things I wrote about actually happened."

"Okay, okay, that may be so," David began, "but I'm telling you, All Terrene is out."

Jason felt a wave of panic move through his body. He felt his heart begin beating faster.

David continued:

"And not just this book, Jason. I mean, All Terrene told me that they are cutting ties with you. Permanently."

Jason suddenly felt faint and had to sit down on the nearby sofa.

"I told you this was a bad move, buddy. The board at All Terrene have labeled you a kook."

Jason then felt a wave of tranquility come over him. He knew this day would come. Catalina and Maria had warned him about it. He felt it in his bones. This was simply a test he needed to pass.

"Well," Jason began, "thank you for trying, David. I'm sorry All Terrene didn't like it. And I'm sorry All Terrene is cutting ties."

David was caught off-guard by Jason's measured reaction.

"You really *are* going nuts, Jason!" David shouted. "You just burned a huge bridge, man!"

"I'm sticking by my testimony, David. I have to share it with the world. It will inspire others to stand firm in their faith."

David laughed into the phone.

"Well, buddy, it's not just All Terrene." He paused for effect. "I'm out, too. I'm not going to enable you. You can't just go from L.A. playboy to Christian mystic in the matter of a few weeks. *Come on, dude.* Give up the game."

Jason took a breath and thought of a response.

"I was lonely in L.A.," Jason began to explain. "The flings and the parties were great for a while, but I was lost. Out of control. I had no compass."

"Oh, poor *you,* " David said mockingly. "All the money and the girls and you're unhappy. You know what your problem is, Jason? You're ungrateful." Jason shook his head and began pacing around the living area.

"I'm not ungrateful," Jason said. "I've realized that I need a true purpose. A reason to get out of bed with vigor. I've realized that I need a partner to share my life with. I've found both."

There was silence on the other end. Jason paced around the room some more while awaiting David's response.

"Well, Jason," David began, "I hope it works out for you, but I'm out." Then the line went dead. David had left the chat.

Jason took a deep breath and walked over to the end table. He set his phone down gently and looked out the front window. Jason steadied his gaze upon the mountain. He felt good.

As the sun set behind Morning Glory, Jason and Catalina sat on the second-story deck and gazed down at the grassy meadow below. Crickets could be heard, their symphony growing louder and louder as night crept over the land.

"So what did your parents and Hernan say about me?" Jason asked while looking out at the dimming mountain.

"They like you," Catalina started, "but they're still skeptical. We *all* know about your crazy days in L.A. You're a known carouser, Jason Morrison. You caroused."

"Sure, I *caroused,*" Jason said. "Past tense!"

"They're not sure why God chose you," Catalina said matter-of-factly. "I mean, you're not pious."

"No… but neither are *you!*" Jason said in a childish tone.

"But I'm not the famous author dude! *You are!*" Catalina snapped back.

"We're in this together, Catalina," Jason said calmly. "Our destinies are intertwined. I think God chose us because we're pure in heart."

His words hung in the air. Only the sound of crickets could be heard.

"I guess it doesn't matter why, just that we were," Catalina reasoned.

The pair sat facing the mountain. Dusk was slowly giving way to darkness. Jason decided to break the news.

"Guess who I talked to today?" he asked.

"David?" Catalina replied.

"Yes… David. And it happened. The inevitable."

"He dropped you?" Catalina said dryly.

"Yep," Jason confirmed. "I've been dropped. And not just by ole Davey. *Oh no!* All Terrene Books dropped me as well!"

"You're kidding," Catalina said sarcastically.

"We knew it would happen," Jason said. "It was just a matter of time. Not if, but when. I'm without representation. I'm without a publisher."

"When one door closes," Catalina began, "many more will open." Her words hung in the air for a few seconds.

"Whoa!" Jason exclaimed. He turned to Catalina and looked at her with a deadpan gaze.

"Did you just make that up?"

Jason tried his best not to burst into laughter as he continued to deadpan Catalina.

"Yes, Jason Morrison," Catalina responded exasperatedly. "I *just* made that up."

Chapter 17

Morning began in a very typical way. Jason lay supine, staring at the ceiling fan, observing his thoughts. He felt both confident *and* apprehensive. His mission was clear, but he knew that there would be obstacles along the way.

"Give me strength, Lord," he whispered as he gazed at the fan.

With that, Jason lifted himself from the bed and strolled to the kitchen. He started the brew process on the coffee maker and made his way to the end table. He picked up his phone and noticed a new text message from Catalina:

Good morning! Can I join you for the Bible reading?

Jason smiled and began typing his response.

Absolutely! Meet me at the stone in five minutes.

As Jason came upon the clearing, he could see Catalina standing in the moonlight. She looked beautiful, per usual.

"Good morning!" Jason said enthusiastically.

"Good morning!" Catalina replied. "So, Grandma Maria told me that you should read from the Letter of Paul to the Romans. Chapter 8, verses 26–30. She said it will help us better understand our roles."

Jason put on his headlamp and opened to the passage that Grandma had recommended.

He cleared his throat and then read aloud:

Likewise the Spirit helps us in our weakness. For we do not know what to pray for as we ought, but the Spirit himself intercedes for us with groanings too deep for words. And he who searches hearts knows what is in the mind of the Spirit, because the Spirit intercedes for the saints according to the will of God. And we know that for those who love God all things work together for good, for those who are called according to his purpose. For those whom he foreknew he also predestined to be conformed to the image of his Son, in order that he might be the firstborn among many brothers. And those whom he predestined he also called, and those whom he called he also justified, and those whom he justified he also glorified.

The concept of predestination had always appealed to Jason. As he grew up, he felt the Spirit guide him toward certain things and away from others. He was drawn to certain people, and knew to avoid others. Jason felt that he was on his own path; for his steps alone. Now, here at Morning Glory, he was beginning to understand what God's purpose for him was all along.

"So this whole thing is part of our destinies?" Catalina asked inquisitively.

"Yes," Jason replied with assurance. "We were predestined by the will of God. To spread our testimony, as well as the Gospel of his Son, Jesus Christ."

"*Pre*destined?" Catalina asked puzzled.

"Before we were even born," Jason began, "God chose us and assigned us our roles. *Pre*birth. Our destinies were bestowed upon us before we even came on the scene." Catalina stood in silence. It was a lot to take in.

"I feel honored!" Jason exclaimed spontaneously. "What a privilege!"

"Grandma said you would like that one," Catalina said with a slight smile.

Dawn was approaching. Jason turned off his headlamp and returned it to the wooden chest. Before closing the Bible, he glanced down at the passage one more time. It resonated with him.

"But I don't feel that special," Catalina stated.

"God thinks you're special, Catalina," Jason reassured.

Catalina let out a small laugh and looked down at the ground. At that moment, the sun peeked over the horizon and illuminated the landscape.

"Did Grandma say anything about the ending?" Jason asked in a slightly nervous tone. "How do we know when our testimony is complete? You know, the end of the story. The end of the book I'm writing…"

Catalina looked up quickly and turned her head to Jason.

"Oh, yeah!" she remembered. "Grandma said that there will be a great fire. Then, on the following day, the final battle will take place!"

"The final battle?" Jason exclaimed. "When were you going to tell me about this *final battle*?"

Catalina looked at Jason with a blank expression.

"Well, you asked about it now," she began, "so I'm telling you about it now. Plus, I didn't want you to fret."

Jason squinted his eyes and pouted his lips.

"A great fire," he began, "and then a final battle. *Interesting*."

"God speaks to Grandma," Catalina said. "She said he speaks to you too. You're tuned in to the right frequency these days." Jason stood in amazement.

"Oh yeah!" Catalina began. "Grandma also says you should send your manuscript to Damascene Publishing. She thinks they'll like our story."

"Damascene Publishing," Jason repeated. "Great name."

That evening, Jason and Catalina sat out on the deck and watched birds fly over the grassy meadow. The summer air was a perfect temperature. Jason leaned back in his chair while Catalina looked through the binoculars.

"Peccaries!" she squealed. "I see a bunch of those hairy little pigs!" Jason scanned the meadow with his naked eye, trying to locate the peccaries.

"They're so *cute!*" Catalina said gleefully, still looking through the binoculars.

Jason continued to scan the meadow in search of the hairy pigs.

"Here," Catalina said, handing the binoculars over to Jason.

She pointed her right index finger to a spot in the grass. Jason brought the binoculars to his face and looked through the magnified lenses. He moved them to the left, then up, then to the right. *There they are!* Jason smiled and followed the pack of javelina with the binoculars.

"Do you see them?" Catalina asked.

"Yes!" Jason responded. "I count four peccaries."

"Ooo!" Catalina cooed. "Do you think it's the same family of pigs we saw at the park?"

Jason continued to look through the binoculars as the javelina foraged through the field.

He was fascinated by their movement; how they moved about in a harmonious pack.

"Maybe," he posited. "Should we take one and bring it back as a pet?" Jason glanced over at Catalina with a slight smile.

"No," she replied, lifting her nose in the air. "I already have a hairy pig… named Jason Morrison!"

Jason smiled and handed the binoculars back to Catalina.

"I sent the manuscript to Damascene Publishing," Jason announced. "All the events that have happened so far."

Catalina brought the binoculars down and looked at Jason.

"I'm so proud of you!" she said.

Catalina threw her arms around Jason and the two embraced.

"Thank you," Jason replied. "I have a good feeling. This story is too good to be kept secret."

As night crept over the land, Jason and Catalina went inside and continued to talk. Jason poured Catalina a glass of wine and helped himself to an ice-cold beer.

"I can't believe you wrote a song about me, Jason," Catalina said seductively while seated on the sofa.

"What can I say?" Jason replied. "You inspire me."

Catalina bit her lip while staring at Jason.

"As a matter of fact," Jason said. "I wrote another new song. Want to hear it?" Catalina looked at Jason approvingly.

"Yes," she replied.

Jason walked through the living area and down the stairs. He fetched his acoustic guitar from the guest bedroom and hurried back. Catalina took a sip from her wine glass and smiled in anticipation.

Jason sat on the other sofa, opposite Catalina. He cradled the guitar in both arms and strummed a G major chord. Then a B minor chord. Then a C major chord. Finally, a D major chord.

"It's called 'See It Through'," Jason stated.

He paused for a few seconds, then launched into the tune:

G   C

Now, Satan's story won't touch my glory

Bm   C

God will see it through

G   C

Hey, Lucifer, you don't have my back

Bm   C

God will see it through

D   C

There's so much you can do

D   C

So much you can lose

D   C

God will see it through

                              G

He'll see it through

G   C

He'd cook the Earth, he'd steal your soul

Bm   C

But God will see it through

G   C

Kill all the plants and animals

Bm   C

But God will see it through

D   C

There's so much you can do

D   C

So much you can lose

D   C

God will see it through

                          G

He'll see it through
Jason strummed the final chord and raised his right
hand. He was definitely inspired.
    "Another hit?" Catalina asked.
    "I think so," Jason replied.

Chapter 18

On the eighteenth morning at Morning Glory, Jason woke with purpose. He hustled to the kitchen and began his routine. Once the coffee was brewing, he hurried down the stairs and went around the side of his house to the western edge of the property. Jason couldn't wait to read a new passage from the Bible. He was a changed man. This was not the Jason of old.

He made his way toward the pine grove and smiled. As he moved into the clearing, he was suddenly startled! There was someone standing by the stone!

Jason recoiled in fright. His heart skipped a beat. Then, he realized it was Catalina.

Jason stood in place for a few seconds, attempting to catch his breath.

"You scared me!" Jason exclaimed. He paused for a moment. "Good morning."

"Sorry," Catalina said apologetically. "I wanted to join you again for the morning reading."

"Let me guess," Jason began, "Grandma recommended another passage?"

"Yes," Catalina confirmed while handing Jason his headlamp and Bible from the wooden chest.

Jason adjusted the headlamp atop his head and pressed the button. *Voila!* Light!

"She said you should read from the Second Letter of Paul to the Corinthians. Chapter 5, verses 11–15."

Jason quickly opened to the book, chapter, and verse, and read aloud:

Therefore, knowing the fear of the Lord, we persuade others. But what we are is known to God, and I hope it is known also to your conscience. We are not commending ourselves to you again but giving you cause to boast about us, so that you may be able to answer those who boast about outward appearance and not about what is in the heart. For if we are beside ourselves, it is for God; if we are in our right mind, it is for you. For the love of Christ controls us, because we have concluded this: that one has died for all, therefore all have died; and he died for all, that those who live might no longer live for themselves but for him who for their sake died and was raised.

"Grandma is very wise," Jason said. "I like your grandma."

"Grandma's boy!" Catalina taunted.

Jason smirked.

"So what's your interpretation of that passage, Jason?" she quizzed.

"Well," he began thoughtfully, "God knows what's in our hearts. There's no fooling God when it comes to matters of the heart. Many people fashion an outward appearance in order to fit in or be accepted. They may say the right things, or do things that are acceptable and pleasing to the crowd… but do they have a place for God in their heart?"

Catalina looked at Jason, listening intently. He continued:

"Living in Christ changes you," Jason stated. "I can attest to that. It's all-consuming. It's practically all you think or care about. You dedicate your life to him. You no longer live for yourself, but for Christ."

Jason looked to the sky. The stars were disappearing slowly as twilight arrived.

"Wow," Catalina said. "I hope I can feel that strongly one day."

"You will," Jason assured her. "You are pure in heart. You're one of *us.*" Jason then opened the wooden chest and returned the Bible and headlamp.

"So what do you want to do today?" Catalina asked.

Jason thought it over for a few moments.

"How about we go to the lake?" he proposed. "We haven't been to the lake in a while."

"Okay!" Catalina agreed.

The pair began their trek down the dirt road on their way to the lake. They came to the gap in the barbed wire fence and passed through with ease. When Jason and Catalina reached the top of the hill, they made sure to stop and take in the breathtaking view.

As they headed down the hill toward the lake, a strange foreboding came over Jason. He was gripped with fear at first, but the fear was soon replaced by a feeling of tranquility. A sense of calm. It washed over his body. Jason sensed something was about to happen.

The duo approached the banks of the lake and stood still. For several seconds, they stared straight ahead over the water. Jason took Catalina's hand and whispered into her ear.

"Don't be frightened."

Just then, a cloud rapidly descended from the sky and came to rest a couple hundred feet above the water. The pair looked on transfixed. The cloud was a dark gray and loomed over the lake. It radiated a powerful energy which both Jason and Catalina could perceive.

Suddenly, a spinning column of air began to descend from the cloud. It touched the surface of the water and moved from side to side in a swaying motion. *A waterspout!* The pair were frozen in place. They tried to step back, but couldn't.

The waterspout continued to drift over the lake at a slow and steady pace. It was awe-inspiring. Jason and Catalina's initial shock gave way to peace. They observed the waterspout without trepidation. Instead, they engaged in its beauty. It was a force of nature.

The spout then began to lift off the surface of the water. The spiraling column of air slowly retreated back into the cloud. A few seconds later, it was gone. Jason and Catalina stood staring straight ahead.

"That was awesome," Jason said wide-eyed.

"Did that just happen?" Catalina asked.

Jason squeezed Catalina's hand ever so slightly and the two stood together. Basking in the afterglow.

As evening arrived, Jason and Catalina sat on the second-story deck and looked to the east. It was a sweltering summer day. The air hung in place with a sticky humidity. Jason noticed how quiet it was. Too quiet. He noticed how calm it was. No birds. No crickets. Not even a passing breeze. It was too calm.

"It's so hot," Catalina said. "I'm going to go in and get an ice water. Do you want one?"

"Yes, please," Jason replied.

Catalina walked around the deck and entered through the kitchen.

At that moment, a light breeze could be felt coming from the west. It was gentle at first, but slowly built to a stiff wind. Jason lifted his head to the sky. Gusts of wind then began to blow. Jason stood up and walked around the deck. As he reached the back of the house and looked west, he could see storm clouds approaching. They were moving at a steady pace.

Catalina walked around the deck with a glass of ice water in each hand.

"Uh oh," she said nervously.

Jason took a glass from Catalina and quickly returned his gaze to the clouds. As he took a sip of ice water, he noticed how dark the clouds were. Darker than gray. As they continued to move closer, Jason noticed that the storm clouds were black.

Gusts of wind continued to move over the land. The tall grass in the meadow below was whipped flat against the earth. A wave of darkness consumed Morning Glory.

"To the other side!" Jason shouted.

The duo moved quickly around the deck as the black clouds loomed over the house.

They felt a few heavy raindrops pelt them as they ran to the other side.

The black clouds continued to be pushed eastward by the strong gusts of wind. A few more heavy drops of rain landed on the wooden deck, but not enough to drive Jason and Catalina indoors. They watched the storm clouds continue toward the mountain, casting a darkness over the land. The pair set their glasses down and moved to the railing of the deck. They couldn't keep their eyes off the storm.

Just then, a flash of lightning appeared! It was a jagged white bolt that came down just in front of the mountain.

"Whoa!" Catalina exclaimed.

Another solid bolt of lightning then flashed before them! A few seconds later, a great roll of thunder. The rain then began to fall harder. Jason and Catalina tried to withstand it, but they were being pelted by the driving rain.

"Back inside?" Catalina asked.

"Yeah!" Jason replied. "Let's go!"

The two ran along the side of the deck and in through the kitchen door. Their clothes were soaked, but they couldn't keep their eyes off the action. They watched the storm intently through the large front windows.

Then, another bolt of lightning came down over the mountain. The lights flickered on and off inside Morning Glory. Catalina grabbed Jason and held tight. A huge clap of thunder followed.

"Ah!" Catalina screamed.

The lights flickered on and off once again inside the house.

"Look!" Jason cried. "There's a fire on the mountain!"

The great bolt of lightning had ignited a wildfire. An orange glow could be seen about halfway up the mountain.

"Oh, no!" Catalina exclaimed. "It's spreading!"

Jason and Catalina continued to watch the wildfire burn along the side of the mountain well into the night. They felt helpless.

"You know what this means… right?" Jason asked.

"The final battle," Catalina answered. "Tomorrow is the final battle."

Chapter 19

Jason woke on the nineteenth morning to the sound of the sputtering coffee maker. The smell of freshly roasted beans traveled from the kitchen to the master bedroom. Jason smiled and sprang from the bed.

"Good morning," Jason announced.

"Good morning," Catalina answered while pouring the hot coffee into two mugs.

Jason continued to the front window. The orange glow could no longer be seen on the side of the mountain.

"No more fire," Catalina said as she handed Jason a cup of coffee. "I told Grandma about the storm… and the fire."

"What did she say?" Jason asked.

"She said, 'May God be with you both'." Catalina paused for a moment. "Oh… and she said you should check your email this morning."

Jason strolled to the end table and grabbed his laptop. He sat down on the sofa and opened it gently. Then he took a deep breath.

One new message… from Damascene Publishing.

"Well?" Catalina asked inquisitively.

"I have a new email from Damascene Publishing," Jason said.

A few seconds of silence filled the air.

"Open it!" Catalina cried. "Open it!"

Jason took another deep breath and read the new message aloud:

Dear Mr. Morrison,

After carefully reviewing your manuscript, we are pleased to announce that we would be honored to be your publisher! We feel that personal testimonies are an essential part of the Christian faith, and we would be glad to receive yours once it is complete.

Please stay in touch so we can discuss the finer details of an official launch and press release.

We here at Damascene Publishing are looking forward to working with an esteemed author such as yourself.

May God continue to bless you and yours.
All the best, Anne Bell

Jason smiled and looked up at Catalina.

"*Yay!*" she squealed as she threw her arms around Jason. "Our story is going to be printed!"

Jason held Catalina tight. He felt great. *What a victory!*

"What are you going to call it?" Catalina asked.

Jason pondered the question for a moment.

"How about… *Jason and Catalina*?" he proposed.

Catalina squinted her eyes and thought it over.

"That *could* work," she began. "A little obvious, though."

Ding! Catalina received a new text message. She grabbed her phone from the counter and glanced down.

"Grandma says, 'Congratulations'!" Catalina said.

Jason chuckled. "Tell Grandma I said thank you."

Dawn was getting closer. Jason was eager to see the destruction of last night's wildfire in the daylight.

"So," Catalina began hesitantly, "are we still doing a reading from the Bible this morning?"

"Of course!" Jason responded enthusiastically. "We're not going to let a little evil ruin our celebration!"

Catalina cracked a big smile. "Good!" she replied. "Because Grandma says we have to read from the Psalms. Psalm 68, verses 1–3."

Jason laughed. "Grandma knows best," he said.

When the sun came over the horizon, Jason and Catalina stepped out onto the deck and looked out to the mountain. Gray smoke drifted over the charred earth, where acres upon acres of trees once stood. They had been reduced to ash overnight.

The pair then moved to the pine grove for the morning Bible passage.

God shall arise, his enemies shall be scattered; and those who hate him shall flee before him! As smoke is driven away, so you shall drive them away; as wax melts before fire, so the wicked shall perish before God! But the righteous shall be glad; they shall exult before God; they shall be jubilant with joy!

Jason was prepared for the final battle. As prepared as he was ever going to be.

"Grandma says the final battle will commence this evening," Catalina said calmly. "Just before sundown, the 666 gang will ride out from the old saloon."

"But I don't have *guns!*" Jason exclaimed.

"We don't need guns," Catalina responded with assurance. "Grandma says God will fight the battle for us. We just have to lure the gang to the stone podium."

Jason nodded. It was a lot to take in. He had faith, but was still filled with dreadful anticipation. *God will see it through,* he thought to himself.

"So this is the final chapter of our book?" Jason asked.

"Yep," Catalina replied.

A few seconds passed in silence. Some birds flew overhead.

"Cool," Jason said.

About an hour before sunset, Jason and Catalina walked out to the second-story deck and began to wait. The old saloon was roughly twenty miles to the south. The 666 gang would ride out shortly.

"Are you nervous?" Catalina asked as she put both hands on the railing and looked out at the highway.

"A little," Jason confessed. "But mostly excited. I'm ready for these guys to go down!" Catalina cracked a smile.

"Remember," she began, "we have to lure them to the stone podium."

"Got it," he confirmed.

Jason then put his hands on the railing and looked to the highway. Soon, a gang of bikers, some of which were from hell, would descend upon Morning Glory. It was inevitable.

Sundown drew closer and the pair remained on the deck, their gazes firmly fixed on the highway. It was a balmy evening. Smoke could still be seen drifting over the mountain. The swath of burned timber was something to behold.

"A great fire," Jason said aloud, "and then the final battle."

Catalina glanced over at Jason. The two looked deeply into each other's eyes. They were ready.

Just then, a faint sound could be heard coming from the highway. The duo perked their ears. It was the sound of engines. Motorcycle engines.

Jason put his arm around Catalina's right shoulder and brought her in tight. They stood together and kept their eyes glued to the highway. The sound grew louder. The gang was getting closer.

Jason then gripped Catalina by both shoulders and held her out in front of him. He stared into her eyes. Then, Jason began kissing Catalina passionately. With the sound of engines drawing closer, the two locked lips one last time before the battle began.

Jason pulled away and looked into Catalina's eyes. She was smiling ever so slightly.

"Let's go," he said confidently.

Jason and Catalina began heading down the stairs on the side of house as the gang of devilish men pulled onto the dirt road. One by one, the bikers revved their engines and headed to the last house at the end of the cul-de-sac. To Morning Glory.

The duo stood at the top of the driveway as fifteen bikes descended upon them. Nine ordinary bikers sporting flame decals. And six bikers from hell, the 666. The men parked their hogs and walked slowly to the duo, forming a row.

They began folding their arms over their black leather vests. They were all wearing wrap-around sunglasses.

Just then, from the middle of the row, there emerged a short man with a weather-beaten face sporting a scowl. His black leather vest was adorned with the 666 patch. He had a gray flat top and was glaring at Jason and Catalina through a pair of Coke-bottle glasses.

It was Bill Banner. The leader of the 666 gang.

"Well, well, well!" the old man shouted. "The writer and his woman. I told you we was gonna run you Jesus freaks out of town."

The gang of men standing behind Bill began to laugh in unison.

"We're *really* scared, Bill," Jason said sarcastically as he took Catalina by the hand.

"You're such a scary little man."

The bikers stopped laughing at once and a look of anger came over Bill's face. The old man grew red with rage.

"That's it!" he said. "You two are *finished!*"

The gang of men flanking Bill stepped forward. They lifted their leather vests and displayed their pistols.

"*Look*!" Jason shouted as he pointed to a spot in the sky over the bikers' heads.

The entire gang of devilish men turned around in unison and looked to the sky. They quickly realized there was nothing there. They had been tricked!

As the gang of fifteen men turned back around, they saw Jason and Catalina sprinting hand-in-hand toward the pine grove at the western edge of the property.

"*Get 'em*!" Bill screamed.

Jason and Catalina continued running at full speed to the pine grove. They looked over their shoulders and saw the gang of men chasing after them.

"We're almost there!" Jason yelled as he gripped Catalina's hand tightly.

The pair were nearly at the grove. The gang of devilish men were giving hot pursuit.

Jason broke his grip on Catalina's hand as the pair entered the grove. They zigged and zagged through the pine trees, moving closer and closer to the clearing. They could hear the devilish men grunting behind them.

A ray of sunshine beamed down on Jason and Catalina's faces. They were in the clearing! The pair quickly hustled to the stone podium and came to a stop on the other side.

They turned around and faced the gang, with the stone podium in-between.

Fourteen devilish men were lined up opposite the pair. Then, their leader, Bill Banner, emerged from the middle of the row of bikers. He took a moment to catch his breath. He adjusted his glasses and began walking toward the stone podium.

"Well!" Bill shouted. "This is the end of the road for you two!"

The gang of bikers who stood behind Bill raised their leather vests in unison, flashing their pistols.

Jason put his arm around Catalina. Bill continued: "No one can save you now!" Bill screamed as he walked closer to the stone. "Not even—"

Just then, Bill's feet began to lift off the ground! The back of his black leather vest was tugged upward and Bill was lifted higher and higher. As if by an invisible hand, the leader of the 666 gang was raised helplessly into the air!

"Let me go!" Bill screamed as he was lifted above the stone podium. "*Let me go!*"

Bill's gang looked on in awe. They were frozen in place.

Bill hung suspended in the air about fifty feet above the stone. He struggled in place as the giant invisible hand dangled him by the back of his leather vest.

"And the one who falls on this stone," Jason spoke aloud, "will be broken to pieces."

At that moment, Bill was released by the invisible hand. He descended quickly and landed on top of the stone podium, breaking into many pieces.

"*Ahh!*" the bikers screamed in terror.

The fourteen devilish men then made a mad dash out of the clearing!

Jason and Catalina stood in awe. They couldn't believe their eyes. Just then, Jason snapped out of his trance.

"Let's go!" he instructed. "Follow the gang!"

The pair ran out of the clearing, being sure to avoid the pieces of Bill that were scattered about.

The remaining gang members moved at a furious pace toward their bikes. They bounded through the field in unison.

At that moment, slight tremors could be felt on the ground. The bikers continued to run in terror, but the tremors grew stronger, knocking some of them off their feet. Jason and Catalina made their way out of the clearing and looked on at the scene unfolding in the grassy field.

The earth began to swirl beneath the devilish gang. It twisted in a clockwise motion, spitting chunks of dirt and grass to the side. The fourteen men screamed in fright as they were helplessly spun around by the swirling earth.

"The pit," Jason whispered.

At that moment, the ground beneath the fourteen bikers collapsed and fell to the center of the earth! The screams of the bikers echoed against the sides of the deep pit.

Jason and Catalina looked on in utter amazement. They were in a state of shock.

"I can't believe that just happened," Catalina said, attempting to catch her breath. "I can't believe that just happened!"

Jason began to walk to the edge of the pit.

"Where are you going!" Catalina cried.

Jason kept walking. Something was drawing him to the edge of the pit. He wanted to look down into the pit.

"Don't get too close!" Catalina shouted as she followed behind him.

As Jason came to the edge, he looked down in rapt awe. It was bottomless. Nothing but a black abyss. Catalina came around his right side and looked down into the bottomless pit as well. The pair stood transfixed. They couldn't take their eyes off the never-ending abyss. Just then, a rumbling could be heard coming from the pit. It was a deep sound, almost animalistic. Then they heard it again. A low rumbling. Like thunder. And then... *a roar!*

From the depths of the pit rose a giant creature! It glowed red in the darkness. It had giant, curled horns. It was the devil himself! Another roar came from the pit as the creature ascended quickly!

"Run!" Jason cried as he took Catalina by the hand.

The pair began to run back toward the pine grove. They ran faster than they had ever run before! Jason glanced over his shoulder and saw the devil's hand come rising above the edge of the pit! The giant red hand clawed its way across the land. Catalina looked back and shrieked!

The devil's hand then grabbed Catalina in a quick motion! Jason tried to hold on, but the beast tugged Catalina away! Back to the pit!

"Nooo!" Jason screamed as he ran after Catalina, who was now in the grips of the devil himself.

The devil's hand moved quickly back to the edge of the pit. Catalina struggled and kicked in his fingers, but it was no use.

At that moment, as the beast's hand was about to go back to the depths of the abyss, a tremendous blade fell from the sky! In one fell swoop, the giant silver blade descended from the heavens and severed the devil's hand!

"Argh!" the creature bellowed as he fell to the depths below.

Back at the edge, Catalina was still in the grip of the giant red hand. Jason ran to her and began to peel back the gnarled fingers.

"Get them off! Get them off!" Catalina shrieked.

Jason threw back the fingers with all his might and freed Catalina. She threw herself into his arms and the pair returned safely to the ground. Catalina's heart was racing as Jason held her tight.

Just then, the pair could feel the earth shaking. Like a mending wound, the earth came together and closed around the bottomless pit, sealing the devil below.

Jason and Catalina held each other tight and looked on spellbound.

"Now *that's* an ending!" Jason exclaimed.